DON'T WORRY
THE SAFETY'S ON

STORIES & OTHER WORKS

THOMAS TIMMINS

ISBN: 978-1-7366334-9-6

Library of Congress Cataloging in Publication Data has been applied for.
Subject: Fiction.

Published by Zoëtown Media

A registered trademark of Zoëtown Media
Greenfield, MA
www.thomastimmins.com

Cover art from Shutterstock.com
Author photo by Kai Winston
kaiwinstonphotography.darkroom.com
Book and cover design by Maureen Moore, The Booksmyth
www.thebooksmythpress.com

For all who've suffered from gun violence
and everyone who is working for gun reform.

CONTENTS

BOOK ONE: DON'T WORRY, THE SAFETY'S ON

Just a Gun

PHEASANT HUNTING	13
JUST A GUN – A PLEA FOR UNDERSTANDING	17
DON'T WORRY – THE SAFETY'S ON	20
THE OLD-TIMEY GANGSTER RAP	24
AMERICA THE BEAUTIFUL REDUX	25
GOD BLESS AMERICA REDUX	27
DIRGE FOR THE PATRIOT SON	28
ODE TO FRANK STANFORD	29
I AINT PACKIN NO GUN	31

Rainmountain and Lasa

THE DUCK	39
LASA	40
AN ANCIENT GROTTO	41
SLUGS	42
EL DIAMANTE COVE	43
BATS	44
LISTENING	45
WAITING FOR THE DRAGONFLY	46
"EL CONDOR PASA"	47
TEN THOUSAND CANARIES	48
AFTER THE AMBUSH	50
THE FLUTE	51

Breathing

BREATHING	55

BOOK TWO: DING DONG CART

Boys and Snakes

FRIENDSHIP, TRUST, LOVE 67
STUCK ON THE INSIDE 68
LAGGARD SPIRITS 70
OWOWOWOW! 71
TICKS, CHICKS, HAWKS, WALMART 73
WHEN SHE WAS A KID, SHE WENT BAREFOOT EVERY DAY 74
THE WAR FOR THE PRESIDENT'S SOUL 75
SKIN 78
IMMIGRATION POLITICS 80
LONELY 81
WRITERS TEARS 82
THE ROSARY 84
VOODOO SPELL 86
EQUINE LOVE 88
BOYS AND SNAKES 91
WALKING WITH A WALKER 93
JANE'S CATERING 95
COME ON, BIG BOY 98
TRAINING 100
DING DONG CART 102
TRYING ON A TRUE SELF 105
A DILEMMA 108
THE TAILOR 110
BRONX ZOO 112
PURPLE CROCUS ON SAINT PATRICK'S DAY 114
HOWZAT? 117

Skeleton Woman

A TRIP TO A FOREIGN LAND 121
SNOW SHOVELING FOR THE GRANDMOTHERS 124
HAULANI TOWN 133

STEPS OR IT'S TOUGH TO OWN A BOOKSTORE   139
WHAT HAPPENED TO THE SKELETON WOMAN, THE HUNTER,
    AND THE INVISIBLE THIRD BEING   143

CREDITS   147
BOOKS BY THOMAS TIMMINS   149

BOOK ONE

DON'T WORRY
THE SAFETY'S ON

Just a Gun

PHEASANT HUNTING

I turned eleven that summer. A few months later, my thirty-three-year-old dad, some of his farmer friends, another kid, and I were hunting pheasants on a sunny November morning in a stubbled Iowa cornfield.

In those days, the harvesters cut the corn stalks down to about 6 inches and left drifts of kernels, intact cobs, leaves, and weed cover behind the combines. A perfect feeding ground for pheasants.

This was my first hunting trip with my dad who was not much of a hunter but he liked to do things with his friends. Most of my farm friends had been hunting since they we in third or fourth grade. I was excited to be a hunter, too.

I borrowed a double-barreled .410 shotgun from my friend, Tony. It was a small gun with two barrels, one trigger. My trigger finger fit just right.

I found myself in the middle of the group, with my dad on my right, trudging across the field, as slow and quiet as we could, eyes up, guns down.

Two pheasant started out of the stover - guns barked. The birds rose into a hail of shot. One dropped. One escaped. It sounded like everyone else had taken a shot while my gun stayed silent and pointed down.

Nice shot, Mel, my dad said.

We moseyed on till we came to the pheasant lying still on the dirt. Its red-masked eye and iridescent green and blue neck feathers and pure white collar above a rusty breast and black-speckled tan and brown wing and tail feathers took my breath away. I'd never been so close to such a beautiful creature.

It was the first up-close death I'd experienced.

Mel picked up the bird and dropped it into a bag hanging from his shoulder. We paused in our trek.

Mel raised his hand to stop us.

"There should be a flock of 'em over the rise where I left a pile of full cobs. Stay quiet for a few minutes until they settle down. "

I was eager to shoot a pheasant. Last week, my dad had brought two home and cleaned them in the back yard. When he gutted them, my brother and I gagged at the stench. My mom cooked them for dinner that night. I liked the gamey taste of the dark meat. We had to be careful chewing every bite so we wouldn't crunch down on a beebee of shot buried in the meat.

As we headed toward the rise in the field, I felt nervous but confident. I switched off the safety on my shotgun and breached the barrel to check that the shells were lodged in place.

Someone shouted, They're up!

I saw them not more than twenty yards in front of me, at least ten birds rising, their wings whirring.

I raised and aimed at the birds and, just as I pulled the trigger, my dad walked in front of me. His head was a few feet directly in front of my gun.

Click.

No other sound came from my gun. I glanced down.

The barrel was still breached. In my haste to shoot, I hadn't pushed the barrel and stock together.

Looking up, I saw my dad rushing ahead with the other men. I stood still, in shock. I'd almost shot his head off.

I started to follow the group, stumbled on a cob, and nearly fell.

As I began to grasp what I'd almost done, my body stiffened. I felt afraid, then embarrassed, then confused, then relieved. I wanted to cry.

I closed the barrel and stock and, the gun now under my arm, hanging by my side, I approached the high-spirited group as they gazed at their bounty, congratulating each other. At least half a dozen pheasants lay on the stubble, some of them jerking, their breasts fluttering and wings shuddering.

As the men chattered, one of the farmers picked up the struggling birds and twisted their necks.

"Mercy," said someone.

My dad looked at me, saying, "Did you get a shot?"

I shook my head no.

"Next time," he said.

I nodded and kept silent.

The field now empty of game, we headed back to the cars, the men marching, talking, everyone, including me, smiling.

"Do you want to carry a bird?" my dad asked me.

"Nah," I said. "That's okay."

I didn't tell my dad this story until decades later. When I told him he was one ignorant son away from dying at thirty-three, his eyes opened wide. After a couple of seconds, he smiled.

"I guess we were pretty lucky," he said.

"It felt like a miracle," I said, thinking to myself, if I'd have killed him, my dad would have been the same age as Jesus when he was crucified. If I'd killed my dad, I'd never have survived to that age.

I never hunted again.

JUST A GUN – A PLEA FOR UNDERSTANDING

I'm a gun. Just a gun. I'm somebody who hangs around. I have a lot of relatives, some close ones like pistols, and distant cousins like automatic assault rifles. They're weird – they all want to be called by the same name, AR15. Like they never grew up.

I don't know how it happened but we are legion in the United States.

We already outnumber people. Pretty soon there'll be more of us than cars *and* people.

I like my name: 9 Mill.

We all have pretty names composed of words and numbers. AR-15, as mentioned. AK-47. Double Ought 30. Glock 17. Remington 1100. If I had friends, my best would be Walther P-38.

It's wrong to blame us for accidents like little boys shooting their little sisters or their moms and dads or those mass murders and suicides and all that suffering.

You can't blame us. We don't do anything. We're just there, here, wherever.

Somebody picks us up and shoots a person or an animal and we get blamed for death. We can't cause anybody to die. We're just things.

By ourselves, we're quiet and peaceful. It's a human who takes advantage of us, using us as weapons.

If we could feel, we'd feel good when somebody dismantles us, rubs good grease around our parts, and slides us back together. We might even feel loved even if some people think we're ugly.

These days we often hear attacks and condemnations, as if we were the cause of blood, mayhem, and death.

Just think about it: me and my cousins, even my weird cousins, we've gotta be innocent. We can never hurt anyone because we don't do anything ourselves. We're passive, even helpless, wherever we are.

If something bad happens and just because we're in the neighborhood, you can't blame us. We've got no legs, no wings, no wheels. We can't crawl. Somebody brought us there and how could we stop that?

One way we're like people is we like to be touched, taken care of, if you know what I mean. In a lot of places, we fly around in pickup trucks and ride in pockets. We can poke

our noses out of people's coats and they're proud to show us off.

With others, we can snuggle in close to their hearts and, yes, to their groins, all warm and happy.

If people want to put us away in the closet or bury us alive or let us rust in the rain, we won't stop them. We can't stop them.

If you could hear us, we'd tell you one thing:

Don't be afraid of us. We're just pretty hunks of metal.

And you know, most people do like us. In fact, you wrote us into your Constitution of the United States of America. Didn't you?

So, we have our rights, just like you.

So, here I am.

Just a gun.

DON'T WORRY
THE SAFETY'S ON

We were all friends, so close that if I said I feel this or I think that it could be any one of us talking except, lately, Robert and Latifa who were beginning to fall away.

They didn't quite match our rhythms.

We thought they stayed around to learn from our way of being so immersed in each other's lives, our individual identities blurred and dissolved into each other, as you may have surmised from what I said before.

Or they, Robert and Latifa, may have had some plan to separate us, fracture us into pieces or shards of who we once were.

I remember Caroline saying, when we were all having dinner in the gazebo at our favorite restaurant, Umbrella Tree, It's unhealthy to live like you're in a nest like ants or a beehive.

We and I didn't disagree. Nobody should live like an ant, we or Katja or I said. We don't always speak aloud each other's thoughts, tho we could.

It may sound to some, like Robert and Latifa, who really should understand better, like we have an ant mind.

Karim said, expressing the other side of the story as she and we often did, Our social arrangements and our scent-based telepathy could help this god-forsaken world so overflowing with guns and sad sack idiots who shoot at other people and themselves.

Rami piped up, The real ant people are the ones with all the guns. If they were like us, they'd dig a hole in the ground and stack all the guns neatly until they could find a way to recycle them.

Killing would drop to almost zero, Trinh or I said.

Bury guns, don't bury people, Jason shouted. Pretty soon, we chanted over and over, Bury guns, don't bury people.

Robert reached into his jacket pocket and pulled out a gun, twirling it around his finger.

Chill, he said. Don't worry. The safety's on.

Kim Chu, Rani, Sam Anugama, Emmy, and I, and we stared at him like he was crazy.

Robert, I and we said in our most soothing voice. Please stop joking around.

This ain't a joke, Robert said, puffing up his chest. This is me. Me. *Me.* Not you, whoever you say you are. Go ahead, live your ant life. You'll never convince me. I'm me, an individual. I think my own thoughts. Sleep in my own bed with my own lava lamp glowing.

He waved the pistol around, not aiming at us. Don't try to bury my gun, he said, then sat down, slumping against the wall.

Take it easy, Robert. No worries, I and we said in our gentle, encouraging voice. You can keep your gun. Just don't let the bee people know you have one. They're on a rampage lately.

Robert looked at us with bulging eyes, his trigger finger twitching.

Latifa knelt beside Robert and caressed his unarmed hand and arm. These are nice people, she said. They're not ants.

They could be larvae, Robert said.

They're grown-ups. You know that, Latifa said.

I'm allergic to bee stings. I don't have a fresh EpiPen on me. I could die.

Put your gun back in your pocket, baby, she said. Let's go over to Camilla's place and make some peanut butter and honey sandwiches. They'll make you immune to bee stings.

Katja offered them a ride in her new electric all-wheel drive F-150 pickup to Bringlino's bodega where they could buy local wildflower honey.

I'll walk, Robert said.

Why don't you ride with Katja? I'll be along when I finish studying the difference between black ants and red ants. I'm almost done for today, Emmy and we said.

I and we watched Robert twirl his gun again, point it at us, then put it in his mouth, sucking at it like a lollipop or a nipple. After a few minutes, his head drooped to his chest and he fell asleep.

Get his gun, I said to Latifa. He could blow his head off if he has a weird dream.

It's his choice, she said as she stroked Robert's head. He can do what he wants.

My and our mouths dropped open.

OK, I and we said. We left them there and headed back to our nest. It was a long and fragrant trip through the grass and along the edge of the wall.

We were halfway down the wall, around the corner from Robert and Latifa, when we heard a loud pop like the crack of a whip or a door slamming.

I'm going back, Womanda, the nurse, said. Maybe he

shot himself.

Maybe he shot Latifa, Rani said, her voice trembling. I and we shivered.

Womanda had turned around and was jogging back. We all looked at Rani. At 6'3" and 300 plus pounds, Rani is our conflict leader. She was the most beautiful woman we'd ever seen. We were proud she was one of us. We started lining up behind her.

Whatever, it was his decision, after all, she insisted.

If he shot himself, I mean, I and we mumbled.

But what if it's Latifa? Rani said. I'm going back to help Womanda. We won't be long.

That felt right to us.

OK, I and we said. We'll head home. Follow the lavender scent. It'll lead you to the door we'll use.

I love lavender, Rani said, scurrying after Womanda. It's so relaxing.

THE OLD-TIMEY GANGSTER RAP

He's a good kid, Ronnie. He does a good job, too.
Yeah, he does a good job.
Too bad he fucked up, Ronnie.

He's a good kid.

He fucked up, Ronnie.

C'mon, give him a chance. Can't you see he's young.
He's trying.

Ronnie, what the fuck did you say? Anybody who fucks
up, anybody who hurts me or mine, that's it.

But ....

Ronnie, do I hear you right? Do you wanna go with
him? Don't fuck up, Ronnie.

Fuck you, fuckhead! He's my kid!

Blam! Blam!

Two men fall dead.

AMERICA THE BEAUTIFUL REDUX

O beautiful for spacious skies and amber waves of grain,
O terrible for specious lies and amber waves of shame,

For purple mountain majesties, above the fruited plain,
For purple mountain tragedies across the arid plain,

America, America, God shed His grace on thee,
Amerigun, Amerigun, who turned Her back on thee,

And crown thy good with brotherhood,
from sea to shining sea!
And crown the hoods with brothers' blood
from sea to warming sea!

O beautiful for Pilgrim feet, whose stern impassioned stress
O terrified the pilgrims' feet whose hopeful passions stress

A thoroughfare for freedom beat, across the wilderness.
The awful walls politicians beat and lost the wilderness.

America, America, God mend thine every flaw,
Amerigun, Amerigun, who could repair thy flaws?

Confirm thy soul in self control, thy liberty in law.
Confirm thy soul in gun control with property the law of laws.

O beautiful for patriot dream, that sees beyond the years
O sorrowful our immigrants' screams, their sadness and tears

Thine alabaster cities gleam, undimmed by human tears
Thine addicts dream, our mother's flowing tears

America, America, God shed His grace on thee,
Amerigun, Amerigun, who turned Her back on thee,

And crown thy good with brotherhood,
from sea to shining sea!
And crown thy hoods with brothers' blood
from sea to warming sea!

O beautiful for heroes proved, in liberating strife
O beautiful our heroes proved by losing precious life

Who more than self their country loved
and mercy more than life.
Who more than self their people loved
but earned no mercy for their strife.

America, America, may God thy gold refine
Amerigun, Amerigun, please your hate decline

Till all success be nobleness, and every gain divine!
Till everyone has open hearts and sees how every person shines!

God Bless America redux

While the storm clouds gather far across the sea,
While the storm clouds gather here and as far as we can see,
Let us swear allegiance to a land that's free.
Let us pledge our lives to make Amerigun kind and free.

Let us all be grateful for a land so fair
Let us all treasure the earth so all may share
As we raise our voices in a solemn prayer
As we open our hearts in peace and loving care.

God bless America, land that I love
O bless Amerigun, land and people that we love
Stand beside her and guide her
We'll stand beside you, rack and slide you,
Through the night with the light from above.
Our rifles raised to the red, white, and blue.

From the mountains, to the prairies,
From the borders to the farms and factories
To the oceans, white with foam,
To the oceans, with all the world's colors flown,

God bless America, my home sweet home,
O bless Amerigun, mi casa, su casa
God bless America, my home sweet home,
O bless Amerigun, our home,

> *mera ghar, bumi abdi, wo de jia.* *

* "My home" in Hindi, Sundanese, Chinese

Dirge for the Patriot Son

The morning the crows landed in the yard,
a fleet of black limousines passed the farm
following the patriot son back from Afghanistan.

The last day of September, the earth was stone hard
from no rain for months. Dry air felt warm
the morning the murder of crows landed in the yard.

Dust rising all around, the limos inched toward the hill,
reluctant as soldiers to disarm
following the patriot son back from Afghanistan.

I leaned against the fence around the vineyard,
the tiny grapes drooping like a wizened charm
the morning the murder of crows landed in the yard.

Twenty thousand bucks for school he'll never see,
a lousy reward. His mother wept with her head on her arm
following her patriot son back from Afghanistan.

Then the birds flocked up at noon, a midnight color guard,
lighting on the leaf bare branch, perched in silent alarm
the morning the crows landed in the yard,
following the patriot son back from Afghanistan.

ODE TO FRANK STANFORD

In honor of Frank, who didn't deserve to die so young.
An imagined letter he wrote to his wife, Ginny, and
his lover, C.D., who were both in the house with him
when the shots rang out.

Ginny, Carrie,
Please make peace. I can't take it and I
have to unload the sheaves and bundles
of pain in my heart.

I'm working to improve my penmanship
so when you read the words.
I'm sorry you're both here. I love you, both
of you are my goddesses, but the goddam
pain's all I feel any more. I don't want you
going down, too, working for money, not
getting your real work done. Besides, my
dreams burn my eyes. I can barely see
either of you now. I'm lost.

So here goes, my baby, my baby, just like
we agreed. I'll stick around in the ghost
world as long as you want me to.
Love forever ....

Frank drew the drapes against a scorching Arkansas afternoon of a summer that came too soon.

He placed his gun against his chest, aiming for his heart and pulled the trigger and pulled it again and pulled it again.

For Frank's beautiful, powerful poetry
see www.frankstanford.com

I AINT PACKIN NO GUN

I aint packin no gun.
Why should I?
You wanna carry a gun?
I wonder why.

My friend Wanda Sue
Lives in the hills up north a way,
She's a nurse, strong, smart, kind, too.
She came to see me the other day.

Wanda Sue, are you packin?
You bet, she said. I wondered why.
I don't carry no gun.
Why should I?

Dont tell nobody now,
She said, it aint legal here.
Up where I live anyhow
Guns're everywhere, just like beer.

Wanda Sue, please tell me why
You're packin that heat.
Your safe around here, that's no lie.
No need to worry you'll get beat.

Wanda Sue said to me, You just dont know.
See that guy sittin right there?
See that bulge in his coat?
He's got a cold, cruel stare.

Wanda Sue, I said, you dont gotta tote that gun.
She said, Course I do. I wondered why.
I aint packin no gun.
Why should I?

It's simple why I'm strappin.
I dont want you, me, nobody come to harm.
Dont you worry bout a thing,
She said, pattin my arm.

I told you, my gun, my faithful one,
My pal, my secret beau.
I dont pack cuz hes warm or fun.
He's not for play, not for show.

Wanda Sue, it aint love for you I'm lackin.
In the old days, I felt safe with you all the time.
Now, with you sittin next to me braggin about packin,
My life dont feel worth a dime.

She said, Take it easy, old friend,
I wont be shootin you.
I'm loaded in case I need to fend
Off some creep, or save some kids, that's what's true.

You're all nervous, shiverin, you're afraid.
Heat's what you need, someone goes on a spree.
That's the whole story, she said.
Me and my 9 Milly, we're strong and free.

I still loved Wanda Sue
Even when she came over hidin her gun.
But I said, Wanda, your packin here makes me blue.
Gotta go, pal, she said. Bein with you, it aint no fun.

You wanna strap a rod?
Stash a pistol in your pack?
Nah, that aint so odd.
It's kinda like bein hooked on crack.

I dont carry no gun.
Why should I, what for?
You wanna pack a gun?
I dont wonder why no more.

I aint packin no gun.
Why should I?
You gonna carry a gun?
Wanda Sue told me why.

Rainmountain and Lasa

THE DUCK

A black duck trills up out of the marshy shore winging toward the sun, curves and skids back onto the lake near Rainmountain's raft.

A drop of water splashes like warm oil on his cheek as a distant bell rings. He rolls over into the cradle of water, sinks into silence, opens his eyes to the algae green world.

He sees his father swim past, machete in his mouth. His father's hair floats straight up, a deep blue flame like the fire that sometimes twists out of El Chinchon, the volcano.

Rainy lolls to the surface. He frightens the duck.

The second it spreads its wings, the machete slips past its heart.

The black duck rises straight up for a few feet, wings stiff, its blood dripping on the water, floating toward Rainy, staining his shoulders the color of pale pink orchids.

Rainy smiles as his father tosses the duck onto the raft, its webbed feet drumming.

LASA

Baseballs of yellow light ripple the air above Rainy's head. In front of his home with its scarred walls, barbed worms tunnel an inch deep in the mud under his feet.

The family cow, whose tongue has been cut our in desperation, roasted and devoured, begins to hiss in the venomous language of winking tree snakes, a sibilant coiling and uncoiling of her throat.

Spotted knifefish in schools burst out of the surface of the river, escaping their cool holes as the river warms and salts with blood seeping from ripped flesh into the shallow churn.

On the riverbank upstream, a shining AK-47 lazes in the velvety arms of Rainy's cousin, Lasa, his only love.

AN ANCIENT GROTTO

Over the ridge, in the tired valley town, Rainy's mother muttered prayers over into the thorn bushes fencing her garden.

His mother raises her eyes into hopeless golden light clouding from the forest like a quivering bank of votive candles begging the Virgin for help in the ancient grotto of her land.

SLUGS

Grey crab, wrinkled frog and orange salamander creatures crawl out of fissures in the mushy earth.

Some emerge wearing brown skins, oily and shimmering. Others appear, a slippery squadron tumbling into the air. Some turn yellow as they engorge on broadleaf ferns, some burn a dark trail across the leaves.

Rainy's feet slide in the grass, his soles greening across the bare roots of a ceiba tree. As he strolls, he blows on his clay flute to keep himself calm.

The slugs begin to steam in the twilight.

El diamante cove

I n El Diamante cove at sunset, cold fresh water seeps from around roots in the cave where Inca treasure once lay, so it was said. Rainy feels cool sand cup his ankles, squirting up as he lopes across the beach.

Swimming to Lasa's raft, he hears buzzing and tinkling. Late light rolls off the water as it leaves the day, wrapping his head in a golden smoke.

Calling out the notes of her name, Rainy throws his lean trunk and legs onto the raft, spraying the chimes, scattering bees from the scarlet zapatón flowers.

He pushes through her beaded door.

Lasa opens her hands, pointing to the mango, the yellow rice, the charred sticks, the basket filled with lime and cocoa.

She smears Rainy's face, streaking his forehead with charcoal, thickening his nose and cheeks with mud. Lasa's art reveals his true face, his death face, his ghost face. Then she smiles into his glistening eyes, "You are a jaguar."

Holding a stub of charcoal like a pencil, Rainy draws on Lasa's face. With his palm he spreads mud on her neck and breasts and over her belly, making her breath catch. His jaw trembles.

Giggling, Lasa and Rainy tumble out of her hut, blinking. Rose cumulus tower over the western horizon.

BATS

Rainy slides between the boulders into the hillside. Thousands of bats flood over his head, out of the cave into air damp and pungent with the smoke blooming from careless burning of green wood.

When Rainmountain discovers the rows of heads, one his father's, hanging, a stalagmite erupts in his brain, heaving gristle, pink steam, every memory of his father holding him, of the miracle of pure suckling in his mother's eyes, his father's growling laugh, bile and blood gushing out of his mouth onto the cave floor.

Furred blue wings sprout from his thighs flinging him outside into a chorus of his friends' screams. He smashed himself against the sky, barely able to breathe through a rising fog.

Rainmountain collapses onto the boughs of the sacred ceiba tree.

His new claws clutch and shred tough leaves, scrape holes in the bark where he tries to bury himself in the soft wood, his knees shuddering and his shoulders torn. He crushes into grease grubs and fire ants into the bark.

LISTENING

Nobody can eat.

Rainy and Lasa and their cousins and families sit by a tentative fire, inhaling the evening mist, listening with veins in their scabbed toes dug into moss like extensions of roots, listening through eyes closed to the drizzle.

Listening through jaws that chew clots of sorrow that cling and won't dissolve.

WAITING FOR THE DRAGONFLY

Macaws and spider monkeys and spiders who weave webs among vines bow as winds gust off the lake, tossing branches all along the shore.

On a sprawling bough in the massive ceiba Rainmountain, thirty feet above a decoy camp, sits with his allies, the spiders and silent birds, waiting to feast on today's sparkling, poisonous Dragonfly buzzing up from the reeking swamps below the dam.

"EL CONDOR PASA"

At the foot of a ruined temple, Rainmountain's cousins build a camp of violet huts with tigerflowers leaning sentry at the meadows edge.

In the center of the camp, Lasa, naked, lies on a flat rock, her cat on her belly purring, a chain of mauve and crimson corn kernels flowing like sweat off her legs. A breeze fans the small fire forcing her to sit and toss her hair as Rainmountain whispers "El condor pasa" over and over and over into his flute.

A scent of sweet innocence spirals up with fragrant smoke luring the Dragonfly's crystal eyes and antennae ears, taunting the droning insect with its hidden soldiers joking in the dim light of its brain.

TEN THOUSAND CANARIES

The Dragonfly approaches, cutting back power, dipping for a look, circling, drifting toward the ceiba, guns drooping in disbelief.

The instant the pilot makes the soft, fatal choice to drop down for a closer look at the naked woman, a yellow screeching storm of ten thousand canaries, flying gluey spiders, and a giant bat dive through the helicopter's open doors, ripping visions of pure control out of the dilated martial eyes, tearing the memory of the last salty kiss out of each small tongue, gashing with beaks and claws the secret longings for love in throats no longer able to hold back sobs, no longer able to cry out.

The chopper howls toward the forest floor spurting thumbs, rosaries, camo pockets emptied of lists of names, a creased photo of a girl with a pink flower in her hair, trailing sapphire flame, choking black smoke.

As the chopper jerks, slamming metallic fury into the trees, it rips open its dark glass, explodes bolts and nuts freed from their perilous duty of flaunting gravity, propellors braided into themselves like suicide ropes.

The mud under her toes sends shudders up Lasa's legs into her stomach. She retches.

The chopper's final thudding, pumping concussion pulls some cousins out of the woods, starting them dancing, spinning, mocking the Dragonfly, and they whirl themselves into the water.

Rainy, gasping, leaps from thirty feet up into the lake where he crashes into a flabby human carcass and sinks it under the waves.

Spider monkeys pitch themselves into the foam on the shore.

Squalling, hooting, the monkeys jump and scramble over floating bodies, seeking the cousins, climbing them and clinging to their heads.

Echoes of explosions ricochet from the hillsides back and forth across the flattened camp.

Lasa, dazed, collects sticks, fragments of canvas, stones bloodied with purple viscera, casting them into the fire, and stands, staring.

Rainy staggers out of the water. He raises his knife to the back of his neck, slices his thick hair, dropping it into the blaze.

The cousins emerge from the water and gather armfuls of yellow feathers. They charge into the forest where the Dragonfly's remains lay folded, clutching at the trees. The pilot sits on the ground, bent in half, lifeless.

When the cousins pile the feathers into the crackling Dragonfly, yellow smokeless flames drift up into the giant ceiba. Its leaves flutter in oily sadness as the children of the forest flee their victory to the caves.

AFTER THE AMBUSH

Coughing in the cave's low smoke, some cousins whimper, some sing to themselves, some fall asleep. Paralyzed in shock, Rainy and Lasa hold each other.

Dense fog rises, merging with the smoke at the cave's mouth, soaking boulders, dripping off the leaves as night closes over the lake.

Rainy watches the fog swirl, mix with the smoke. He feels it mix with Lasa's sighs, mix into the quiet in the cave. He blinks away faces of the dead soldiers who look like his cousins and him.

THE FLUTE

The wreck smolders and sputters nine days, nine nights.

When moist wind spills down from the hills, stirring the ashes and the scars of the camp, Rainy's flute, abandoned clay, groans the death loss into the wind.

Breathing

BREATHING

I should have known better but even if I had, would I have stayed home that night?

How could I have stayed in, the very day I learned everybody every day breathes atoms of the Buddha's eternally recycling body, that same day I decided to put on my good luck black pearl earrings and take my breathing practice into the suffering world, the same day I heard the inspiring story of the beautiful wife of the famous preacher who loved him more than thirty years as much as a woman can, giving him four children, standing behind his every preacherly and political move, loving him while keeping her own identity as herself, even when that beloved man fell in love with a young widow and made with her the baby she and her now dead young husband never got around to having, and if that famous preacher could make a baby with the young widow when he helped her rebuild her life because she was too young to grieve her youth away and too lovely to avoid the yearnings of men of all ages and too weak to bear any love but the preacher's whose heart brimmed with compassion until after hours of inhaling the pain of her sorrows he came to know her as a woman of passion whose fragrance intoxicated him as if he were a teenage rector again sneaking sips of the communion wine after evening services, if he and that girl could make that baby and bring it to his family home to his wife whose soul must have wings, sharing it with his other four children and their spouses and two grandchildren and if the mother of all of them, that spiritual woman, accepted that baby and she must have encouraged everyone to hold that new baby she had no blood tie with so the baby could inhale their love and then exhale its tingly baby breath over them with purity and innocence that baptized them with gratitude nobody could have predicted when they first found out last year that the famous married preacher had a lover and she was pregnant, oh yes, if that beautiful spiritual woman and all her children could be so brave and accepting, I could, I would, and I did take my mindful breathing practice out of my meditation room into our suffering world by strolling down Beresford Street at eleven o'clock one late August night wearing my white flowered skirt and my white cotton blouse from Guatemala doing my Buddhist breaths of compassion, inhaling the unknown and the spaciousness surrounding the nothing from which everything arises, exhaling the vapors of a star, inhaling atoms breathed by dinosaurs, exhaling peace, light, and any relief I could offer, ready for anything the void presented me, prepared to know nothing about how to respond to violence I might witness, to drugs I might be offered, to my own terror at being approached, as I was, by three men who demanded that I come with them or they would have to drag me by my bitch hair so I went with them inhaling their desperation and letting it mingle in my chest with the roots of a raw scream that I exhaled instead, unable to run because two of them trapped me between them and they pushed me into a garage where I gave them my cheap watch and my crystal teardrop necklace and they ripped my black pearl pendant earrings off, tearing my earlobes, and I inhaled my own agony like iron nails in my jaws and exhaled musty relief when they cheered the two hundred twenty seven dollars they found in my purse before one shoved me down onto a greasy, muddy floor but not before he ripped off my shirt, tearing it like paper in his grimy hands while he slobbered on my neck with saliva that smelled like cat shit, and I didn't know what to do so I exhaled the sweetness of light onto his scabby bald head, even when he pushed my skirt up and yelping like a stepped-on dog he yanked my panties down and dropped his pants and lay on top of me and just lay there waiting for something to happen, I inhaled his decayed teeth and I exhaled my wild heart pounding in my ears and I gasped for air and exhaled so shallow when the other men laughed and said leave that bitch we got what we want you can't do it no way so let's go and they both spit on me and the man laying on me grunting and exhaling his excremental breath into my nose slapped me and cursed me fuckin bitch shit cunt and he rolled off me and staggered up pulling his pants on kicking me many times but I didn't feel anything and he stumbled out of the garage while I lay there exhaling peace and health and purity and light and inhaling greasy sour sickness of heart and lung and clogged pores and rotten food festering in tumorous guts and then I stood up finally and wondering what to do I pulled my long skirt up to my shoulders so I was covered with a short dress, and then nausea rose up into my head and I bent and retched and retched and I leaned against the wall with my stomach clenching until I pushed away and I dragged myself back to Beresford Street shaking and shivering with warm blood still oozing down my neck from my shrieking earlobes and I inhaled deeply the garbagy scent of poverty and the broken streetlight colors of shadows and I exhaled the calm of a damp, earthy garden of tomatoes and corn growing right there in a vacant lot in the middle of the city and I opened myself for the next thing that would arise from the void and still not knowing any better what to do but feeling quite the blessed girl inhaling and exhaling, inhaling, exhaling, inhaling, exhaling, I staggered home and climbed into the shower, letting the scalding water scrub his reeking touch off my skin, inhaling my honeyed soap scent, exhaling gushes of tears until I fell soaking wet into bed and sobbed and sobbed, inhaling the sea scent of my tears and exhaling my searing hate for those creatures who could have killed me and I sobbed until I slept and woke up and called Ronnie and asked her to come over and sit and breathe with me because my body wouldn't stop shaking and shivering until she came over and kissed me and I inhaled her minty breath and she inhaled my soggy ashen terror and we breathed and cried together and I hammered my fists into the bed until we broke down laughing and rolling around and then we got serious and she held me for a long time and we talked and talked and I understood the world in a new way and I decided if I wanted to practice my breathing in the suffering world, I'd better buy a gun and learn to shoot it before I went out to Beresford Street again, and I would, I wanted to, and I did learn, thanks to those three rotting slabs of men who tore tear tracks into my earlobes that I'll wear till I die, I will be ever thankful because I started shooting practice, inhaling metal polish as I aimed and exhaling fully before my finger inhaled the trigger so my hand stayed steady as my pistol exhaled its deadly breath and I ripped my target heart shots again and again, always inhaling the blue light of peace and exhaling the dingy smoke of my own imperfections of mind, body, and spirit before I pulled the trigger, calmly inhaling burnt sulfur fumes and exhaling misplaced joy in my power, concentrating on the object of my aim, hearing the crash of the shots pass like galaxies being born, watching the bullets eat emptiness into the paper chests of my targets, I became a Marksman faster than any other man, woman, or policeman ever did at the city range, with a license to carry my Ruger P920 as naturally as I carry groceries, breathing in whatever fumes the void presents, exhaling my fear, my imperfections, inhaling all the stenchy and intoxicating scents of this murky realm, exhaling my loving breath into the eternal wind that blows its perfume everywhere life is, everywhere death is, and returning it through me as I inhale and exhale the mysteries of this rank and fragrant world.

BOOK TWO

DING DONG CART

Boys and Snakes

FRIENDSHIP, TRUST, LOVE

You don't know me yet, but we'll get acquainted soon. I have nothing to hide but I know some things about you. Jeannie told me how you eat only gluten-free fettuccini and never wear your war medals in public.

You maybe don't know Jeannie and I were a unit when we worked at Costco, she a clothing folder, me a check out guy.

Now she's yours and you're hers and none of us wants it any other way. She's trustworthy and I think I am, too.

Even so she maybe never told you about the time she asked me to crash her car for the insurance. I did it, nobody got hurt, and when the claim settled, she gave me five hundred dollars. I needed it back then. We were good friends.

Now she doesn't need to tell you that. No secrets between us all. The air is clear for us to meet. You know I still love her and she loves you and I'm not the jealous type. I only want what's best for her.

Stuck on the Inside

As you can imagine, everyone was sick of it. The inner life, y'know.

It felt like that unlit cave we learned about in some class or book somewhere. Not that we were trapped. We had flashlights in our hands and a line we carried in from the cave mouth. We borrowed the line from a construction site so it was a little frayed, but not to worry, really.

Mostly we missed the expansive view of anything in color, outdoors, indoors, anywhere. In that cave when we turned our bodies and heads around to find anything interesting, we saw the same thing – a yellowish glow from our flashlights projected on a smudged dusty screen of emptiness.

Until Mahmoud Gomez taught us how to concoct things called "images" while listening for musical sounds. All we had to do whisper to ourselves random combinations of numbers like "652" and "814" and "198" and try to see them in the gloom.

Mahmoud said they all had pleasing vibrations.

I was improvising my best when next to me, Brin started screaming. On the other side, someone started pounding on the wall. At that moment, I saw a huge bonfire with ten or twelve men standing around it, drinking beer, smoking.

Every now and then, one of them stepped away from the group to swing their cudgels at the ground again and again so fast I heard the squeaks of grass ripping and the deep bass groaning of beaten sod.

Brin's screaming morphed into sharp screeches so loud I turned off Mr. Gomez and stroked Brin's shoulder in the dark. She heaved and sobbed, "I gotta get out. I gotta get out."

"Brinny," I whispered, "open your eyes. Look at me." She calmed down a little, whimpering. "Remember, I said we'd go shopping when we got out of here?"

She wailed and slapped my hand away. I understood how she felt, because I felt the same way, only, she wasn't afraid to express herself. I've always been known for my self control.

Brin and I had been into the inner life for three weeks already. We didn't know how long we'd stay there but I felt sure we'd make it. We had plenty of food and water. When

we ran out of supplies, we expected deliveries of more. If we got too bored and all else failed, we could turn to Mr. Gomez and work on the images.

LAGGARD SPIRITS

T hen a spider leapt up on a boulder.
A black bristly thing with tiny glaring ruby eyes.
Its legs contorted around its body almost denying
its noble eight-leggedness.

The spider sat there, still, posed on the gray-green
lichen on top of the waist-high round stone.

He'd walked toward the park entrance earlier, but because of a masked couple, speaking intently, and trudging along in front of him, he turned back to the other entrance where the unfortunate spider lay in wait.

He picked up the spider, crushing its six-inch body and foot-long leg into his jacket pocket.

This was the morning after Halloween when some of the infernal spirits missed the carts and wagons that return them to the other worlds.

Left behind, the laggard spirits cast off their material bodies then hide in the shadows of trees and rocks and in people's fears and prayers in the parks and inside cast-off plastic spiders.

Except for the children who forget about the spirits until the adults remind them again this time next year.

Owowowow!

When I heard Willsyboy, my five-year-old neighbor from three houses down, wanted to ride his bike up and down my steep driveway, I was flattered. He's seen me riding my bike up and down, always grinning. He must have noticed how happy I looked.

Sometimes I glide down from the garage, turn up the street then turn right around, pedaling as hard as I can to feel the momentum push me right to the top of the driveway.

When I get there, I stop, dismount, and holler Owowowow! three times.

The other day, another neighbor, Karuna Radewagen, heard me hollering my victory cry.

He popped his head over the fence and said, Hey, Georgie, wanna come over, watch a game?

I looked at him without speaking.

He continued. I like your war call. What's it? 'Owowow.' Besides, I'll enjoy the game more if someone is in the same room cheering on the team when it's twenty-seven points down with seven minutes to go and we still have a chance.

I stared at him.

It sounds like a losing cause, I said. If my team was down so much I'd be weeping.

No, no, don't worry, Karuna said. Twenty-seven points to these guys is like one point to everybody else. I'm a fan. They've got the best shooters, the longest hitters, the farthest passers, the fastest runners, the hardest heads. They usually let themselves fall behind so they get a little challenge. They're 43 and 0 for the season. If they don't win by 20 points, they feel they betrayed their fans.

That's different, I said. I'll come over and 'Owowow' with you after I change out of my biking clothes.

He looked at his phone. Game starts at 8, he said. Don't worry. I've got two six packs of that pilsner you like.

I didn't care about the game, but I liked my neighbor. I looked forward to talking with Karuna about the state of our trees and whatever happened to Moshe Braun, the roofer, since he fell of his ladder and broke his collar bone. I'd try to get excited enough to do a victory cry because Kaurna's such a friendly guy.

Tomorrow, I'll invite Willsyboy over to cruise up and down my driveway with me. We'll ride together and I'll teach him how to sing out the Owowowowowow! as loud as he can. And pump his fist ten times!

Ticks, Chicks, Hawks, Walmart

They're not very smart, she said, referring to the month-old guinea chicks. But they're voracious bug-eaters. It won't be long before they scratch and peck around my whole yard and clear it of every tick, grub, ant, anything that crawls in the grass.

By then, they'll be full-grown. Even if they squawk all day and keep us up all night, we protect them so we can mow the grass without worrying about getting tick bit and sit in the yard evenings to enjoy the twilight.

What about bobcats and hawks? I said.

Kim has a rifle to shoot the hawks and scare away the coyotes. Bobcats, too.

Good idea, I said. A yard without ticks is worth a dead hawk or two.

I've seen few red tails circling already, she said. See you later. We're on our way to the Walmart for ammo.

When she was a kid, she went barefoot every day

At 95, she sat on the deck chair in the breeze.
"I don't need a blanket," she said.
"Don't you feel cold?" they asked her.
"Only in my heart," she said.
They tucked her in a wool blanket, smiled, and retreated.
She watched them disappear into the house and laughed.

THE WAR FOR THE PRESIDENT'S SOUL

The President was a known gambler. Only last week, he'd made a fortune by taking the Chinese premier to the cleaners.

Today, on a campaign visit to the New Bedford Marina, he eyed his opponent's paltry $100 ante and laid his own $100 bill on an upended lobster trap.

The President made his bet: If he lost the game, he'd sell his soul for an hour to the fisherman from Fall River who put up the fishing boat he'd inherited.

1, 2, the President said.

On the pier, the President's gambling rival, wearing rubber boots standing across from the President, pulled his Navy watch cap tight to his ears.

3, the President said.

The fisherman covered the President's fist rock with his palm paper.

The fisherman grinned.

Don't worry, Vlad, the President shrugged. I'll keep my Secret Service around. They protect me, no matter who owns my soul.

In a spirit of a good winner, Vlad offed his ante to the President. He took it and handed it to his Chief of Staff.

By the way, the President said, what plans do I have for my soul in the next hour?

Eyes watering, but alert as a gull at dawn, Vlad considered.

Well, sir, he said, his gimlet eyes on the slight depression in the President's forehead where his third eye never grew in. First, I make an NFT of your soul. That way I'll have the thing for the more than an hour. I'll post it on Facebook. Then I get famous. After that, I probably sell it on eBay or Craigslist or someplace.

The President wrinkled his brow.

Then I'll be rich. And famous, Vlad explained. Like you. With how famous you are and all, I expect a record bid. Bigger than for a dead President, that's for sure.

The living President smiled, glad to hear he'd hold another world record. He'd always kept his priorities straight, despite what he called his 'penchant to wager big'. It shot him from Silicon Valley to the White House in less than a decade, almost as fast as Obama made it from Illinois.

Make sure you get paid with some crypto, the president said. I hear it's finally going up again.

Mr. President, you are a smart and honorable man, Vlad said.

Good luck, Vlad, he said as the Secret Service fetched the Presidential bullet-bomb-and missile-proof Hummer. Where I live, stupid beats smart but clever beats stupid.

Vlad nodded. I heard that one. Don't luck beat clever, though?

Sometimes, Vlad. Sometimes, the president said in a wistful tone. Let's put off that hour till later. My schedule is a little tight today.

Sure. You're the Chief, Vlad said.

The President headed toward the Hummer. He put his

hand on the door handle, hesitated, looked across the forest of masts in the marina, then turned around to face Vlad.

How about one more game of rock scissors paper? Double or nothing. Two hours of my soul for your boat?

Vlad whipped his hand behind his back.

In a split second, a smile crossed the President's face. He loved a challenge and right now, he would face the battle of his life.

Hold the car, fellas, the President said. I got a battle to win.

SKIN

My skin is breaking down, Melany said. I've always taken care of it. I mean, the skin on my whole body, not just my face and hands.

I'm sorry to hear that, Jess replied, sipping their tea, relaxing in the booth at the coffee shop. Have you seen the dermatologist?

Melany leaned forward. Did you know your skin is your largest organ?

Jess shrugged.

I bet you thought it was your brain.

Jess winced, then smiled.

Imagine if you peeled it off –

Jess tried humoring them. You mean like, scalp your skeleton? They shivered.

It would cover your living room floor!

Ghoulish, Jess said, sliding over and standing up beside the booth. We just had breakfast. You're upsetting my stomach.

Look here, Mel held up their hand. A tiny pimple reddened a finger knuckle. And here, they said, pointing to her knee.

Jess leaned over. Is that a bruise? Did you bump into something?

Mel went on. You should see my belly button. It's starting to glow.

Let's see.

I'm not showing you in public.

Jess raised their eyebrow. Later then?

Sure, they said, ticking their camera app, offering them her phone. Would you mind taking some pictures of my neck.

Jess shook their head. You're twenty-seven-years old. Nothing's wrong with your skin. I gotta go.

As Jess left the café, Mel peered at her phone, then took half a dozen selfies of her head.

Unsatisfied, they turned to the woman in the booth behind who was dipping a donut into her coffee. Mel smiled and said to the woman, Could you help me?

IMMIGRATION POLITICS

U p the street from the new Cumberland Farms gas station with a Subway and Dunkin Donuts, the lunch brands I am fond of, the American Legion threw a party last night.

Josh and I happened to be walking by discussing how sad it is that nobody seems to understand that war never stops, not just for the brainwashed soldiers but for all of us.

We understood because we'd been in Iraq, Nigeria, the Philippines – 12 different peacekeeping missions for the Marines. We were the trainers of the native soldiers who ran the drones and lasers from the battlefield.

They called us The Middle Men because sometimes we were on the ground in the middle of a battle showing the guys how to retrieve a downed drone. We wore impenetrable, indestructible suits that hid our body heat from prying android eyes.

As we passed by the building, we thought the illuminated sign that said "The American League" was an office of the baseball business. When half a dozen men and women, everyone wearing helmets and the women in high heels, shuffled out the front door shouting and toasting "Victory! Number One!"

We realized were seeing a small crowd of old veterans who saw the most action of their lives decades ago.

Josh stopped a woman who wore her gray hair in a long braid to find out what the party was about.

Edward

Bridget (Hynes)

Patrick

Theresa

Jenny

Kathryn

Minnie

Thomas

Lena

Margaret

She said, The General's coming to explain why we should let immigrants in.

We think we should keep them out, she said, but we're open-minded.

She turned to the red-faced man standing behind her.

Carl, isn't The General's idea immigrants will make good farmers and workers. They could clean up melted wax on the machines in our local Yankee Candle factory. Bernice told me they don't mind that perfumy smell either. It's nothing compared to where they come from.

I hear The General has a bunch of them working in his country club running the kitchen, Carl said. They make great caddies when The General flies his buddies in from Washington, Iraq, wherever.

Josh pointed to a woman across the street with an AK-47 slung over her shoulder.

I walked up to her and asked if she knew how to fire the gun.

Sure, she giggled. Simple. Just lean against a tree or a car, aim, pull the trigger.

This bothered me a little. I asked her another question. Does The General let you carry the guns into his speech?

He can't stop us, the other women said, sounding offended. We can do any kind of carry we want – open, closed, both. Anyway, there'll be police cruisers and some National Guard here. They might bring some artillery. I'm sure we'll have at least one drone circling around up there.

She pointed the barrel of her gun straight up and bounced it up and down circled it around as if she were flying a kite.

We know about drones, I told her. Don't think they're magic.

LONELY

At 59, he's tall (6'4"), fit (runs 50 miles each week), married (second time, for eight years now), father (one boy, one girl, both moved out of town, now living in Chicago), broke (doesn't care, he says), lonely (Carol told him You need friends), contemplating therapy (analysis sounds a lot more appealing than the physical release probings), addicted to middle of the night movie streaming (horror, sci-fi, old dancing, comedy, and shootemups with Astaire, Chaplain, Eastwood), sleepy (too much TV), lonely (nobody else within ten years of his age can keep up with him on the trails and streets), lonely (at the lake he watched a Canada gander terrify a collie who was a quarter mile away from his goose and eggs), lonely (Carol took her three-week vacation this year with girlfriends), lonely (his favorite song is "Only the Lonely" and Roy Orbison is dead), lonely, lonely, lonely.

WRITERS TEARS

J udy and Stan, highly recommended pest controllers, took care of my rat problem in two short days.

Their victorious hooting like two barn owls as they drove off with the booty reminded me of the pigeon who rules the big hay mow.

After that, I didn't know what to do with myself until the Captain arrived saying, At it, soldier!

I dropped to the floor to give Captain Dorsett fifty pushups and a hundred gut crunches he always demanded.

When I stopped crunching at forty-seven, he said, "Son, don't overdo it. This is the modern army, but even we don't need hyped-up, testosterone-sucking grunting geezers–even if you work for free! Go on home, lad. Curl up with a good book and enjoy your irresponsibility."

Always a good listener and well-trained student, I followed the Captain's order. Called up my girlfriend, Thalia Book, invited myself over for a shot of Writers Tears Irish whiskey.

My fate, my good luck, my reward: her fireplace was glowing, and now here we sit, sprawled, really, on her wide black leather couch, all cuddled and warm, sipping whiskey, listening to glowing oak logs crackle and whoof.

THE ROSARY

T oo late, the door closed and John, or Juan, as they called him, kissed Wendy saying, If it doesn't feel like sunshine all day, I'm a horned toad.

Wendy turned away before kneeling down on the grass to tie her new turquoise sneakers, *Bound to Rise* brand, Limited Edition.

Lifting her head up, still on her knees and using her Thai wood bead bracelet, she began to pray the rosary, an old habit lately returned for no good reason. Once she's accepted the habit, when she prayed, she felt shivers, then the drive to love and help everyone.

Her life swung from the surreal to the real. The Virgin Mother watched over her, she could breathe again, and Juan, the sweetest wanna-be cowboy in Austin, the old-fashioned gentleman, asked her to marry him, no conditions attached, not even a pre-nup to protect his oil and tech stocks from her perfidy.

I hope it works, she thought, knowing her history with men, men not her forte, she never could understand them outside the bedroom or the kitchen.

Her fingertips rolled the smooth cool rosary beads in an infinite loop, round and round. Wendy began to weep, smiling at a memory she couldn't quite grasp, but it was a happy one, almost as happy as the one she was making now.

VOODOO SPELL

ome in here, Germain. The last cup of that good hard cider is waiting for you on the coffee table. Bring me my bottle of Gordon's, will ya? It's gotta be half full.

As usual Harry acted like the boss of the apple sauce. Germain flicked flies away from the jam-spotted counter.

Try another channel, Harry. Or else turn it off. I can't stand seeing all those people stuck in a room like pigs in a truck. I can smell 'em. They stink.

I like the laughs, Harry said. Anyway, a voodoo guy is comin' on. I don't want to miss hearing him talk about the zombies he's met.

Germain slid a chair over next to Harry sprawled on the couch. I never thought you'd turn out like this. You used to be so active. You're starting to act like a zombie yourself.

She fiddled around in her purse, pulled out something, and opened a large safety pin. She raised it in her hand, then brought it down, jabbing it into Harry's thigh.

Harry screamed. Aaaaaaaa. Jesus Christ. That hurt. You dumb ass.

Across the room, skipping out the door, Germain cackled. Great. You're gonna thank me for that, you dumb ass yourself. That's a anti-zombie spell you got on you now.

EQUINE LOVE

When she left for church I told her, I'll find your mare after we get home.

I'm not worried, Bobby, she said. Vicky's smarter than most people.

We'll see, I said as we got in the car to head out to the ranch.

Outside the barn, we sat and propped ourselves against the south wall, enjoying the sun. I'd unpacked two fresh bales of hay and spread them around the front gate. Then I made a path of oats leading to the stable.

At dusk, Vicky returned all lathered up.

I told you, Bobby. All we had to do was wait.

We watered her, dried her neck and flanks while we talked to her. Then she went right to the oat bucket inside her stall in the stable. She was the queen of the ranch and she knew it.

The young stallion at the far end of the stable kept his eyes on her, sniffing and pawing the ground.

Soon, he lost his mind, snorting and neighing shrilly. He rose up, pawing the air, and pounded the wall of his stall with sharp hoofs, shredding it.

I tried to soothe and calm him with words, but he kicked at me, baring his yellow teeth. I had to shoot him with horse tranquilizer. He sighed and stood silent, looking at me with sad eyes.

She said, Bobby, you shouldn't interfere.

He could rip the barn wall apart trying to get at her, I said.

I don't think so. She's tougher and bigger than him. Besides, what's a new barn wall?

He could knock over the whole barn.

She'd handle him before he did that.

I'd have to go into town for the boards and the horses would have to hang around in the wet paddock.

Building something would be good for you. You don't have anything better to do.

We watched the young stallion, William Goldstone, for a while. He shook his head back and forth, up and down, whinnying non-stop.

The mare, Vicky Blue, snorted and pushed open her stall door, then sauntered out through the barn door into the paddock.

William Goldstone stomped the hard dirt of his stall, still confused. He lifted his nose to the top of his stall, whinnying as if he was screaming. I thought he felt rejected or abandoned.

I approached him with a bucket of water and a pail of oats. He looked at me, kicked out, and tossed his head. Eventually he drank.

Vicky Blue nosed open the paddock gate and wandered out to the pasture.

BOYS AND SNAKES

Worship

A statue of a bone-white serpent lying and laughing under the slippers of a serene blue and white Virgin Mary adorned the side altar of St. Patrick's drafty old church in the little town on the prairie.

Fear

Randy Matt revealed that the fearsome buzz sawing from the spreading oaks and tall locusts whose boughs hung over the sidewalk came from snakes dangling from each tree waiting to drop on us and wrap us around our necks and strangle us with their thick shadowy bodies.

Birth

My cousin told my brother and me about it. We ran across the neighbors' yards, across lawns, behind houses and sheds, climbing a mossy rock wall. She lay in brown grass basking in the July afternoon sun, a mother snake curled around a wet slithering heap of snakelets.

Study

While riding their bikes, the eight-year-olds discovered a dead brown snake on the path. They carried the animal on sticks to the garage where they lay it on a flattened cardboard box and chopped its body into slices. After studying the snake chunks, they slipped them one by one into plastic baggies. They labeled each bag – "Guts," "Tail," "Head," "Scales," "More Guts" – and lay the bags on a picnic table. They called to their families to come see their science project presentation.

Death

Toney spotted a garter snake behind the barn. We caught it, stepped on its tail, crushing it into the dry grass, clubbing it with sticks until we stunned it still. We stabbed and skewered it, lifting it up, one of us from the tail, one from behind its head. We draped the green scaly thing through the fork of a branch we found and planted. The snake lived, shivering and spasming. So we pumped it full of BBs from the guns we carried when we wandered the woods. We shot the snake until we ran out of BBs. We knocked the pulverized thing to the ground then we stomped on it again, tearing it apart with our sticks and shoes, smearing its guts under our feet in the dirt. No more blood flowed. We tossed the carcass over a fence and forgot about it, till now.

Walking with a Walker

5:44 p.m. Hiking trail

Brilliant sun. Dozens of lizards basking on cracked mud. I'm in a rush, so I hike as fast as I can up the steep meadow, across mown hay, sidestepping thistles and hacked fennel. Gophers have quarried the whole field. I step on a soft heap of crumbled earth, first one foot, then the other.

Sweating, hustling back down, I meet a happy young family, smiling mother, dad with sleeping infant on his back, a three-year old girl who grins and calls up to me Hi!

They hike on by and I pass through a mirror in my mind of me and my babies thirty years past.

7:39 p.m. The auditorium

I stop the car beside the curb and see Sally heading up the dim steps.

I shout, Sally, can you watch my friend while I park? I get out of the car and help my ninety-nine-year-old friend to stand.

You're nuts if you think I need watching, my friend says.

Maybe so, I say, but you'll love Sally.

Sally takes my friend while I park.

Inside I ask the attendants, showing my cash for her ticket, Did you see a little white-haired lady with a walker?

No, she said.

I show my badge and hustle past, my eyes scrolling the

crowd. There she is, near the center aisle.

They'd rolled her and her walker up the ramp, bypassing the ticket-takers.

When I catch up to her, she says.

Walkers get in for free, grinning as if she'd won the lottery.

7:55 p.m. The auditorium

Sally's quizzical eyes fastened on my aged friend as I settle her and her walker. She hadn't expected to see my ancient companion.

I say to her, joking, Juanita had a time-warp experience this afternoon. She went somewhere and came back 35 years older.

If I look like that at ninety-nine, Sally says, I'll take it, walker and all.

JANE'S CATERING

L ast night Jane stopped over on her way home from the Community Dinner.

It was the worst I ever had and I been goin' the last two years, she said to my wife Martine and me. The cherry juice was so sour it gave me a canker sore. Here, look at my lip.

Martine peered into Jane's stretched mouth, nodding.

Jane suddenly stood up. I gotta go. Tomorrow morning we're doing the Chamber of Commerce breakfast. I hope it turns out better than tonight.

What are you serving? Martine asked while I helped Jane on with her coat.

The usual. Scrambled eggs, bacon, toast. That kind of thing. Maybe some yogurt and fruit.

I dunno for sure. Depends on what Max scrounges from the supermarkets tonight. He knows all the night managers. They give him deals on the stuff they usually throw out. It's still good, she said giving me one of her hard looks.

Good luck, I said. Let us know how it goes.

As we watched Jane climb into her van and back out of our driveway, Martine said, What do you think of her slogan?

I read aloud, Jane's Catering: If you don't want leftovers – don't call Jane's! I don't know. It's catchy, but what does it mean? She's been in business, what, two weeks?

Martine walked over to the kitchen sink and washed her hands. Are you going to the Chamber breakfast tomorrow?

Nah, I think I'll stay home and have my usual oatmeal with maple syrup. Did you forget I gave up bacon? Pork chops, ham, too.

After you watched that cooking show, right?

They butchered a pig. When they hung it up, I couldn't tell the difference between the pig and a human body. Or what I think a skinned human body looks like. Makes me sick to my stomach right now just thinking about it.

Martine gave me a sympathetic look. She was used to my sensitivity to everything – cat hair, molds, greasy cooking smells, even wood smoke. I'm surprised we're still together – nothing bothers her. Maybe that's why.

Oh yeah. We watched that show with Jane. That was when she got her idea to go into catering.

Jane's as tough as you, I said.

She's stubborner, Martine said.

Okay. That's enough about Jane, I said.

Jane is one of those people who drains the air out of my lungs if I'm around her more than a few minutes. I'm always happy when she leaves. I moseyed into the kitchen where I opened a new jar of gherkins to go along with a hunk of peanut butter.

Ignoring me, Martine said, Cheap is king with Jane. And just about everybody else around here. It won't matter if her food is fresh or not. She'll make it just fine in catering.

Come On, Big Boy

Waiting to fly out of Rochester, I watched passengers file past my seat, wishing for a small quiet man to sit beside me so I could doze beside the window.

Today I got a large, pretty woman wearing a blue suit and white sneakers. She barged between the seats, banging my head as she situated her briefcase on the floor and her body into the seat.

I hope I don't embarrass you when the plane takes off, she said, bumping my shoulder while she downed two yellow pills.

I'm not a good flyer. I run the aisles. I scream. I'm going to take a course in airplane noises. We had an emergency landing in Buffalo. All I could do was shout My condo! My condo! Last week the pilot came back and gave me wings. He gave me wings because I was so calm that day. I fly three times a week.

The plane pulled out and rolled down the runway. As the pilot poured on the power and the plane roared toward

takeoff, she groaned, leaning into me as she gripped my arm.

Come on you sonofabitch, you sonofabitch. Get up you sonofabitch. Come on, big boy. Get up. Come on! Do it, baby!

Once we were in the air, she ordered a beer, gulped it down in a few swallows, leaned back and floated off into her own clouds. After a few minutes, her eyes popped wide open. She squeezed my arm again, hard.

How was I? Not bad that time. I know I'm getting better. Wait till the landing. You'll see how good I really am.

TRAINING

She found me in the barn that rainy afternoon but if she 'hadn't found me then and there,' she said a thousand times, she'd've have found me by the stream or at the church.'

She'd been listening to me 'prowl and howl for weeks' she'd say. 'With ears like mine, I couldn't help it. I could even tell if your paw was hurt,' she'd simper to me.

'I could hear your limp in the way dust settled back onto the hay. I could hear the pain in the satisfied little mew you like when you crack a mouse's bones. My minister's teaching would never let me ignore you. Sweetest one,' she murmured again and again while she stroked my back.

'There's tuna, chicken liver, cream from Old Bossie, and pure cistern water.' She intoned the morning menu while she picked through last night's chow. 'You can't avoid them maggots. It's a farm, you know. If your little mind insists you feast on fresh mouse and not the nutritious food I give you,' she whispers, 'well, maybe we can't let you out to prowl and howl anymore without a leash,' as she buckled a sequined collar around my thin gray neck.

'O, it's the wild ones like you I love to find and train.'

She rocked in a chair creaking like a stuck door. 'I love to hear the muffled patter of your new clawless toes,' she said as I run and leap and pull against the collar and, as she reminded me every day, 'of the inevitable suffering in this harsh world.'

I climbed on her lap and then sprang off, choking and falling to the hard wooden floor before she laughed and hauled me up by the leash to her lap, where I caught my breath, waiting for her to fall asleep.

DING DONG CART

I visited the sprawling country of marriage, met a lovely woman there, emigrated, fell in love, got hooked, became a citizen, bought property, settled down until the July the men with trucks finished work on our new house.

The same month the news flew around town that a new ice cream shop, The Ice Cream Emporium, had opened up in the ruins of the old roundhouse a few towns over.

My wife wasn't interested in traveling so far. But I, eager for chilled sweets and old-timey fun, collected my new neighbors and we piled into my van to cruise on down, planning to try new flavors – Barbershop Mint, Maple Street Swirl, Nutty Neighbor Bars, Flat White Coffee.

We pulled into town. We stopped a woman walking along and asked for the Ice Cream Emporium. She said, 'You mean Rice's Crematorium. It's real famous, just down the block. You oughtta check it out. It's got a cool history museum – wood pyres, pressurized heaters, smokeless stoves, recorded rites from around the world.'

Pointing at something behind us she said, check out that sign.

Ashes to Ashes
Rice's Crematorium
Portable Pots
Your choice - Brass, Ceramic, Crystal.
100% Dessication Guaranteed

No way, we said, let's get outta here.

We followed the road out of town back across the border into the forested country of work, that vast northern highland near the mountainous region of my destination and home, the happy nation of family I knew we'd find out soon and we did.

Pennants flew from the houses, wild carrots and garden petunias sprouted among the cemetery headstones and alongside the streets.

As we approached from the distance, I heard the children chanting to our local Ding Dong Cart's twelve-note chime with its again and again and again promise of Old Fashioned Vanilla, Strawberry Galore, and the O My Gosh Chocolate nobody can resist.

I floored the accelerator, headed straight home.

I apologized. My bad, I said to my new neighbors.

No worries, they said. We had a good time anyway.

I dropped off the neighbors, picked up my wife, found the kids, and drove back to where I heard the Ding Dong cart.

We followed the music as it moved through the town, its tune becoming fainter and fainter.

Faster, Dad, my daughter said. I sped up, listening hard for the chimes of the cart. I turned and turned and turned again, getting lost.

Forget it, Dad. Let's just go downtown to the I. C. Shoppe. They have more flavors than the Ding Dong.

So, I forgot it and took the family downtown.

TRYING ON A TRUE SELF

Too many showed up again though nobody complained.

The air felt fresh enough, maybe a little moist. The breeze helped. We stood with our backs to the wind, telling fishing stories. None of us fished, but we had friends who did, so we repeated their specious tales of triumph, and laughed.

I went home early and called Kayin. She'd just sold the house she'd lived in for at least 45 years, where she lost her husband and her daughter's ex-husband. The ex was one of the richest men in the county whose health gave out early.

Kayin had told me she'd never worry again since she'd lost not only the husband and the ex-son-in-law, but her post-husband boyfriend who sold golf equipment. He followed the sun. Kayin never knew what he was up to in the winter since she stayed up north to be with her grand-kids. They didn't ski but they played in the snow and baked brownies.

Kayin picked up my call, said, Thanks for calling, Dayo. I'm doin' fine. Happy.

Glad to hear that, Kayin. I was worried about you since you cried all yesterday afternoon.

I'm over it. Just crying because I was remembering the best times of my life when my kids were little. Now I'm glad to get out of there. The place had too much sun for me. I'm living in the woods now. Marie and I are getting married.

What? Marie? You're getting married to a woman? You're living off in the woods? I said. Do I know you anymore? This is not who you are, Kayin.

Maybe it is, Dayo, she said. I read a book about true selves and false selves and ….

I interrupted her. Was it by the guy who wrote *You be You, I be Me*?

I dunno know, Kayin admitted. Anyway, I'm trying out a few different selves. For now, I like this one, the happy one living with giant trees all around me. Gotta go.

Wait, I said.

She waited.

Invite me to your wedding. It's been a long time since I went dancing.

Who said anything about dancing? We're doing it in the kitchen while we make fondue and drink wine. It's a cabin, for Pete's sake. There's no room for dancing.

I really wanted to meet this Marie and check out Kayin's place in the woods. I was getting tired of suburban living myself. Well, I'll just stop by with flowers to celebrate, I said.

Kayin's loud sigh grated in my ear. Dayo, you know I'm allergic to flowers. That's one of the reasons I like the woods

– moss, lichen, bushes, jack in the pulpits. Maybe I can find magic mushrooms. Stop being so pushy, Dayo.

I was about to apologize when she said, I'll call you sometime, then she hung up.

I didn't blame her for cutting me off. I'll be patient. She once told me when she and Jerome got married, they couldn't go on a honeymoon because they both had to work and save money for the baby. The baby they were saving for turned out to be the daughter who grew up to be the girl who married the rich guy and who gave her her first two grandkids.

Kayin is always so responsible so this living in the dark woods with a strange woman didn't bother me too much. When she comes down from the honeymoon, she'll call and we'll get together. I know her real self real well.

I remembered how pretty she was when we were young and neighbors. I don't know how it happened but one summer afternoon she gave me a haircut on her porch. Maybe she was thinking of going to work in a hair salon and I was one of her guinea pigs. I don't know if the haircut was any good, but it didn't matter. It was fun.

Other than that, I don't recall much about those days before I moved to Oklahoma for eleven years then came back and lived across town. I liked Jerome and Kayin and their kids. They were a lively family.

One of their boys sold me a car I drove for quite a while before a wheel fell off when I turned the corner by the Recovery Center. I don't know if it was because I didn't keep up with the maintenance or because the car had something wrong with it when I bought it and it was just waiting to collapse. At least it happened in a quiet part of town and nobody was hurt.

A DILEMMA

You should keep this car, Jerome, said Bo from the darkness of the back seat.

Yeah, Dad, said his daughter, Melody, from the front passenger seat.

You've had a lot of cars, Bo said.

I have, Jerome said, chuckling. All of them old.

I can't even remember all of them, Melody said.

I can't either, Jerome said. My first one got towed but it leaked so much oil, I didn't bother retrieve it.

I woulda kept it. I know this girl who can fix anything on any car.

I didn't know anybody like that. Besides, it was my first time in the city.

You should keep this one, Bo said. It's a good one.

I like it, Melody piped up. It doesn't smell too bad.

If you want to get rid of it, give it to me, Bo said. I can fix it up. I'll sell it and split the cash with you 50-50.

I'm going to keep this one a while longer, Jerome said. But when I'm ready to let it go, I'll tell you.

Don't wait too long. I heard the girl, her name is Ayana, might be moving to Queens. I might not know how to find her.

Jerome sighed. He was tempted but he didn't have any extra money to make a down payment on a new car. The kids fell silent. Soon they were asleep. Jerome drove on into the night, meeting cars that always had brighter headlights than his.

THE TAILOR

The tailor told me my clothes would be ready by Friday. I forgot about them till yesterday. I went back to his shop. I dug out my ticket and laid it on the counter.

Hi. I'm here to pick up, I said.

OK. What is it? Mr. Haldi said.

I smoothed out my crumpled receipt. The dark blue tuxedo and a sport coat, maybe something else.

He turned to the rack of finished tailoring and fished among shirts, pants, a few dresses, sports coats. Empty-handed, he came back to the counter.

Sorry, sir, he said, peering at the illegible receipt. We gave them to the shelter. We thought you'd be back but after a year, we had to clear our racks.

But I paid you already.

Sir, he said, shrugging, you can write it off your taxes. They went to a good cause.

I grimaced.

All right, Mr. Haldi said. We'll give you something, a nice substitute. It's black. Better.

He opened a dark wooden door behind his sewing machine where a dozen or so cats lounged in a large cage.

Jumbo. Jumbo, he called, reaching into the cage, picking up the largest black cat I'd ever seen. Come to Baba.

When he held the cat out to me, I said, No way. I rushed

toward the door, stopping for a second in front of a floor length fitting mirror to look at myself. I'd lost some weight. I spotted the tailor behind me, pushing the cat toward me.

Sir. Take Jumbo. I have something else for you, too. Please come back to pick up.

He held up a green and white checked sport coat I recognized. It was like something I wore when I was into fooling around at the clubs. Those were some crazy days. Best in my life.

I walked back to the counter, reaching for the coat.

Sorry, sir, the tailor said. You can't have one without the other. Cat. Coat. Coat. Cat.

We stared at each other. Without losing eye contact with me, he wrapped the coat around the cat and held the bundle out to me.

I took a deep breath, wondering what to do. Then grabbed the bundle and dashed out.

BRONX ZOO

She said she'd always be my friend, and friend she was. She knew that's what I wanted, that's all I wanted.

We were in the park, after work, after the people, the workers, the students, the homeless had all gone someplace else. The maple trees with their red leaves surrounded the park and us, a wall of scarlet flickering in the breeze at dusk.

That's what I wanted to hear, I said.

Do you believe me? she said.

I don't know, I said, but it doesn't matter if you're my friend or not. I will always remember you.

She said, Believe me. I'll always be your friend.

The bus arrived. She hoisted her backpack, kissed me on the cheek then on the lips. I hugged her, sliding my fingers into her hair and stared into her eyes. They were wide and round, deep brown, damp and shimmering.

We smiled and she climbed aboard. When the bus pulled out she waved from the window and I waved back.

I got on my bike and pedaled through the gap between two enormous maple trunks, down a tunnel under thick branches. It wasn't long before I was home.

I went inside, turned on the kitchen lights, poured a glass of Malbec, then went out on the porch where I sat in my yellow Adirondack rocker. I felt something, a stiff envelope, in my pocket.

I opened it with my fingernail and extracted a card about the size of a playing card. A lion's face gazed at me without animus or curiosity. It was a black and white photo.

I turned it over and read it. 'I'll always be your friend. I took this picture at the Bronx Zoo the summer we met ten years ago.'

I propped the lion's face against my good luck rock on the little table and sipped my wine, rocking slowly. She would always be my friend. I had no idea if I'd see her again, probably not.

I wish I'd remembered to give her the card before she left.

Purple crocus on saint patrick's day

All I wanted was to become a medic, a Good Samaritan under fire, offering what I thought was a high service. Not as high as the priesthood but close. And it would have made me a hero in my eyes, and my mother's showering of prayers would have graced me with God's will to keep me alive.

The draft board, an ancient, now defunct organization comprised of loyal Americans dedicated to providing fodder the Army in the 1960's, said I wasn't a patriot, in fact, in their eyes I was a traitor because Catholic boys always went to war and killed the enemies. I should go to Sioux Falls and join the other good boys.

I became an exile, a felon, a war resister, an expat, a draft dodger, a hero of another kind in my and some of my peers' eyes.

I'd just begun to adapt to living in the underground (we called it) culture of war resisters and peacemakers when the U.S. Government found another role for me in the Post Office. This was before anyone could have found out about me on the internet.

First, I took the civil service exam. I was smart in those days, a couple of years out of college, so I scored at the top of the class.

The job I wanted was a part-time rural route driver, but it went to a woman, an older woman, as it should, I thought, since had a mother, a wife, a daughter, sisters, girl cousins. Though my female competitor scored lower on the test than me, I was happy she got the job, that the Post Office was at the forefront of hiring women for what used to be men's jobs.

Another Post Office job came up, so the next month, I found myself a U.S. Government employee in uniform, without a gun, but with a beard and unkempt hair, tossing boxes and sorting letters.

As a young father living with wife and baby and working at the U.S. Post Office I was only a mail clerk but we paid the rent and ate well. Those mornings before work at the Post Office, at 5:30 I ate oatmeal seasoned with apples, almonds, brown sugar, yogurt – the original health food.

Later, at work, as I settled myself on my sorting stool, memorized the addresses and sang quiet songs to stay awake. My young body shifted around to make myself comfortable and keep me from falling asleep. I'd stand, then sit sideways, then lean back, then turn around and sort over my shoulder, then prop myself up on one leg.

Until the Mail Room Supervisor, a tall, red-faced, choleric World War II Navy veteran, had enough of my insubordinate way of being and sitting and sorting. He stalked out of his office, fuming, and screamed – "You! Sit on your goddam stool the right way!"

My friend and fellow sorter, Tommy Martin, a Korean war vet, was embarrassed, while my other clerk colleagues smiled, amused and entertained, the boredom of sorting demolished for the day.

That afternoon, St. Patrick's day, March 17, as I walked home, I saw purple crocus blooming outside the town library and realized it was a sign I could be free, take the risk, quit the freakin' Post Office job that had carried me and my family through the winter. So, I gave two-weeks' notice.

My last day as a Post Office employee was April Fool's Day. That day, my wife and I celebrated the fertile spring and our freedom to dig up our lawn, plant a garden, be outside all day long if we wanted. Nine months later our second daughter was born.

Howzat?

Lemmee hear whachee said?
Din't say nut. Why'a wanna hear't innyway?
Cuz she's talkin' bout her.
She's alright. Sed he liked'er tits. Donchu?
Yeah I guess. I like her.
The door opened.
Sup withat?
Wind, musbee.
They waited but nobody came in.
Less head down fr' snack. Nuggets?
You gofer d'crap they call chickin? Gums my teeth.
'Sgood fer ya innyway.
Gimme aminute. Checkin' my texts.
Whya awwees doon' nat?
Dono. Habit. Might see somethin good.
Less go.
Looka this. Watta mess.
S'all yers. I'm hungry.
Alright.
I'm gonna see som'n good, too.
Cool. Like, what?
Like, who gonna rub my feet.
Rubyer feet? Wut for?
Big wart on my sole. Hard t'walk.
Ya can't rubba wartoff!

Yeah, ya can. I'll teach ya. Take off yer shoes.

Sox too?

Putem ona bed. Lay down. Relax. Tend yer fallin asleep.

Ok. Jis my feet.

Mebbe I'll do yer ankles n'achilles.

Gonna use cream, er oil, er som'n?

Ya wan coconut 'rolive?

Coconut. Like d'smell.

Yeah. Ok. Howzat?

Tickles.

Zat?

Jeez. Yer handser freezin.

Ya wanna rub er not?

All cool. Take't easy.

Howzat?

Oooo. Sweet. Swee-eet!

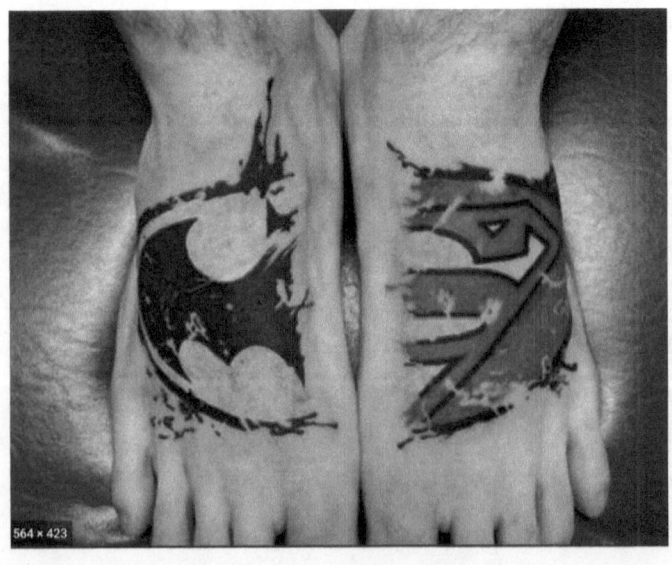

118

Skeleton Woman

A TRIP TO A FOREIGN LAND

I f you've never tried it, you should visit another country. You'd be surprised what you can learn.

I went over the border one day, just started walking around looking at the people and houses and stores and signs. I couldn't read anything so I thought I'd see if I could connect with a local.

I asked a well-dressed man if he could tell me the time. I pointed at my wrist where I used to wear a watch and said, Sir, do you have the correct time?

He stared at me and said in English, It's time for you to learn my language, pal.

He hurried off leaving me puzzled about why he was so unpleasant. I was dressed properly. Everyone has always told me I'm one of the politest people they know.

A couple of teenage girls came my way so I smiled my friendliest and said, pronouncing my words with precisions, Excuse me, young ladies. Would you happen to know what time it is?

They stared at me, then giggled. I tried again, this time speaking louder. Was teem iss eet? I pointed at my wrist then the sky and said,La sola maybe uno or dos or ...

The girls jumped back, grabbing each other's hands and ran away giggling. Looking back at me and laughing as they skipped down the sidewalk.

I realized I should try something different. I sat down on a bench beside a fellow who was slumped back and with his legs stretched out in front of us.

I opened my pack and took out an apple, holding it out to him on my palm. His eyes lit up as he snatched the fruit and whistled. Now I'm getting somewhere I thought. He pursed his lips and whistled again. My ears rang.

A large bay horse trotted toward us, his shoes clopping on the street's bricks.

Time to eat, the man said in English as he offered the apple to the horse who plucked it up with his prehensile lips and chewed a few bites, then sauntered back to where he came from.

The man slouched down on the bench, pulled his hat over his eyes and seemed to sleep. I'd had enough.

The way they treated visitors. I wondered if they'd act any nicer if I were an immigrant. From what I'd learned, I doubt it. I decided I knew what time it was – time for me to cross back over the border and do a post-mortem of my trip.

I learned a few new things: If I hadn't made the journey, I wouldn't know so many people speak English. The smile that makes people relate to me like a nice guy might be scary to foreigners. Whistling to horses works the same over there as here.

When I told my friend Gina about my trip, she grinned, rubbed the hair on the top of my head, and said, Silly boy. Next time you go, download the translator app. Those people will love it.

But I didn't need it. They spoke English.

Well, then, she said, you can pretend you don't speak English.

Astounded, I shook my head and felt a foolish grin invade my face.

Let's go get some of that new soft serve ice cream, she said. It's only 53 calories per serving.

All right, I said. I'll take two. I'm hungry.

We began heading to the Dreemo store when a thought occurred to me.

Remember that country I just came back from?

Yeah, she said, you just came back.

Well, I want to go again someday. Do you know how to count in their language? It would help me a lot on my next trip.

Gina laughed. Come on, she said.

Snow shoveling for the Grandmothers

The mayor wrote me on Sunday morning. She told me to go out to the street with a snow shovel and a bucket of road salt.

A group of Kenyan marathon runners' grandmothers was visiting and they wanted to explore Meadow Lane, my street, the only street in town with three-story Victorian houses.

A wintry mix of snow, graubel, ice, sleet, and rain was scheduled to fall about the time the grandmothers planned to explore the neighborhood. Nothing can stop those grandmothers, I thought. No wonder their kids and grandkids win all the marathons.

Then the mayor texted me saying to make sure I brought a broom along with the shovel and the bucket. She said the grandmothers were prize-winning horsewomen and would be riding dancing Palominos.

As a homeowner, she said, you should be proud to shovel and salt and shovel and broom for the grandmothers and the reputation of the town, no matter the weather.

I grasped her subtext right away – our town did not have a good street plowing force. We had two trucks that took days after a four-inch snowfall to clear the streets. The town council wanted to host a marathon next year so the mayor marshalled the residents to show off our readiness and tidiness.

I don't know if I was proud, like the mayor said I should

be, but I liked doing my job as a citizen.

The snow piled up on the road while I shoveled a path from one property line to the other. The freezing rain started. I tossed salt on the street, hoping it would prevent ice. Nobody wanted a horse to slip and fall with a grandmother aboard.

My neighbors, who were salting and sanding the street in front of their houses, and we hollered to each other as the rain drenched us.

I've never been to this rodeo, called the Rose, the jokester who lived next door on the east as she tossed sand across the width of the street in front of her house.

Frank, the guy across the street to the west, a curmudgeon and constant complainer about property taxes and the schools, stood in half-a-foot of slush with no shovel, no sand bucket, no broom, shouting, You guys are suckers. There's not gonna be a marathon. No world class runner will show up in this boondock!

He trudged back to his house and stood on his steps, watching, as curious as any of us suckers. He lived up to the

nickname Rose's kids had given him: Frank the Crank.

It wasn't long before I heard what sounded like sleigh bells and the clip clop of horses' hooves on pavement. The sleet and rain changed back to fat flakes, exciting me even more. What a day for a parade, I mumbled to myself. But the show must go on. I scooped and tossed to keep the path open as the wet snowfall thickened into a gelatinous curtain.

Rose joined me in opening a trail past the Crank's house. We couldn't see more than ten yards through the snowfall, but the other neighbors in both directions seemed to have shoveled. Like us, good neighbors and conscientious citizens.

The insistent sound of hooves came closer. At that moment, the snow let up, the rain stopped. Out of the dim daylight, a caravan of matched Palominos, their platinum manes decorated with red ribbons, their necks straining forward, slogged up the hill toward my place on the plateau.

Tall, elegant women, decked out in regal rainbow colors, swayed on the horses' backs. Their soggy gowns glowed gold, scarlet, emerald, blue. The women smiled at me and blew kisses as their horses sashayed by.

The heady perfume of a kitchen redolent with baking butter and caramelized sugar pastry drifted down from the grandmothers, filling my heart with gratitude for the unexpected memories of my own sweet time with my grandma Cora.

Following the grandmothers, a couple of local farmers' muscular dray horses hauled a wooden farm wagon up the hill. The mayor and her cohort sat all bundled up and huddled in their heavy down jackets and wool hats.

I wondered why none of the mounted marathoners or

wagoned politicians had opened umbrellas.

As I waved to the passing dignitaries, I heard a sharp cry up the street behind me, near Frank's property. I turned to see the last woman's horse flailing, its legs sliding sideways. Every time it pounded a hoof to balance itself on the icy street, another leg would slip. The grandmother riding tilted and twisted to stay erect, but she tipped right out of her saddle and plopped into a snowbank beside the street. Her turban flew off into a hedge and she flapped her arms up and down as if trying to rise like a bird.

Good thing we'd shoveled Frank's section of the street into a snow heap, I thought. Not so good we forgot to spread the salt.

Frank, who'd watched the parade from under his porch roof, leapt down the steps, pushing through his mushy yard toward her. When he reached her, he took her hands, pulling her upright. I'd jogged over to see if I could help. When I was only a few feet away, I saw her dark eyes flashing. In pain? In embarrassment?

She cried out in her language, flung Ralph's hands away. She stamped her feet into the slush, splashing it up into Frank's face, and shuffled toward her horse.

He stood grinning, mesmerized like a kid who knew he did something bad or maybe it was good, but he wasn't sure which.

The parade of grandmothers, still and silent now, all the women turned around to see what happened, looked like the colored and lit ice sculptures the town showed off during its winter festivals. Then one of the Palominos clomped its hooves. Another mimicked it. Soon all of them tapped out a clomping harmony, splashing slush.

The riders moved and swayed with the rhythm the horses kept. Sweat on the beautiful animals' withers streamed down their front legs but none of the horses moved ahead. A few snorted, maybe impatient to get the circus back on the road or maybe disgusted with their jobs right then.

Who knows what horses think? They must think.

The fallen and now risen grandmother faced Frank and clapped her hands. He jerked out of his stupor and slogged over to her. Her white hair was styled in a thick coiled braid that had come undone so it flowed down the back of her soggy sapphire gown.

She signaled Frank to come closer. He had no idea what she wanted but his grin widened. He trudged over. When she lifted her arms and grasped her saddle and lifted her boot, he gawked. She said something I couldn't understand. Frank frowned.

Letting the saddle go, the grandmother turned to him and seized his hands, forcing him to bend while holding his hands together. He leaned there, trembling, his hands dangling in front of his knees.

The grandmother nudged her horse closer to Frank whose cringe I could see from across the street. She stepped into his clasped hands and lifted herself into the saddle, settling her heavy robe around her.

Frank stayed bent over until she patted him on the head with the toe of her boot. When he looked up, she pointed to her turban in the shrubs.

His befuddlement, obvious as he trudged in the snow, snagged the turban from the bush, leaving a long gold shred dangling.

He offered the torn and flattened turban to the grand-mother who shook it out and settled the soggy thing on top of her head.

Facing forward, the grandmother clucked, and the parade started moving. The grandmother's long hair hung down like a phosphorescent cape as she swayed in time to her horse's gait. My neighbors watched it swing back and forth like a hypnotist's pendulum.

As if the whole scene wasn't strange enough, the grand-mother's body started shaking and bouncing in the saddle.

I broke out of my mental fog, fearing she was having a seizure until I heard her laughing. Her horse kicked up its hind legs, and all the grandmothers started laughing. They sounded like a chorus of kids having the best time of their lives.

Frank came out of his trance and turned to look at me, a goofy grin on his face, something I'd never seen before. He raised his arms in a what-happened gesture. Seeing him posed like that triggered a burst of happiness in me. I doubled over and laughed so hard my belly hurt.

When the mayor's wagon passed, I was still laughing. I noticed she'd shrunk into her bulky coat, holding her hands over her face. Everyone in the wagon seemed to be dazed.

We watched as the parade toiled up the final rise and disappeared around the curve and started down the other side of the hill. Our little coterie of shovelers gathered in front of Frank's house to share this once-in-a-lifetime experience in our neighborhood.

After chatting for a while, we noticed the grandmothers' mounts and the farmer's horse had left memorial gifts on the street. Happy to be of service, we scooped up the steaming biscuits in front of our houses. Rose invited us to toss our prizes into the compost pile beside her garden.

The grandmother's horse left an especially large memento for Frank. Minutes after we'd cleared our parts of the streets, we clustered together, leaning on our shovels, wondering and gossiping about Frank's exchange with the grandmother.

When he emerged from his garage pushing a wheelbarrow with a shovel in it, we cheered. Rose, laughing and clapping, called, Bring it on over here, Frank.

He scowled but rolled his wheelbarrow to the street.

In silence, while we watched, Frank scooped up then dumped his historic load of horse manure on the compost pile. Good job, Rose said. That's enough to fertilize my tomatoes next summer. I'll make sure to bring you some in September.

Frank muttered Thanks and pushed the wheelbarrow up our horse-fragrant street to his house.

A few weeks after the incident, though the grandmother wasn't hurt and they'd told the council they didn't hold the grandmother's fall against the town, the Kenyans passed on scheduling a marathon with us. On our street, we expected that. When others in town learned of Frank's role in causing the grandmother to fall, he became a pariah, shunned in the grocery stores and, sadly, at church. Even the librarians ignored him. Sunday school teachers used his refusal to be a good neighbor as a moral lesson about what happens to others when one person shirks his community duty.

Still, one of our progressive town councilors stayed in touch with the Kenyan grandmother she'd struck up a friendship with who happened to be the grandmother who fell off her horse. The Kenyan woman showed us all what personal grace and nobility could do to overcome possible disaster.

She told our councilor that the parade through the snow was the highlight of the Kenyan grandmothers' tour of U.S. towns. She mentioned how pleased she was that the man had helped her climb back on her horse. He was so funny when he stayed bent over, he reminded all of the grandmothers of a baby rhino.

One of my neighbors had videoed the entire scene from the beginning of the rather somber ride until the grandmothers disappeared into the snow shower, their laughter bubbling and echoing through the neighborhood.

When the councilor sent her friend in Nairobi the video, the grandmothers found it so hilarious they posted it and spread it across the Kenyan internet. The grandmothers became famous.

The grandmother friend helped arrange a foreign exchange year a couple of our high school kids did with a couple of Nairobi kids. At the end of the first year, the foreign exchange parents from the US and Kenya visited each other. They revealed to everyone they had a tough time convincing their children to come back home to Kenya or America.

On our side, the Kenyan kids taught US kids how to run long distances cross country in any weather. It wasn't long before our kids won so many races they became the envy of the high school athletic conference.

Of all the consequences of Frank's churlish behavior before the parade, his total change of life affected us all more than anything else. After the town's ostracism, he felt so humbled and ashamed, he asked the town councilor to put him in touch with the grandmother so he could apologize.

He emailed his regret and told her what had happened to him. She sympathized and forgave him, and an intercontinental email courtship began. Ralph traveled to Nairobi where he met her children and grandchildren and sisters and brothers and friends and fell in love with the grandmother. He sold his house across the street and moved to Kenya.

The grandmother helped him set up and run a Kenyan fabric design and export business. Within a few years, Frank and our enterprising mayor had turned our town into a fashionista suburb of Nairobi and put us on the state's tourist map like no marathon ever would have.

When wedding invitations arrived from Kenya to Ralph's old neighbors with tickets for a private safari to see giraffes and hippos and wildebeests – and rhinos – every one of us accepted except Shakir and Makawee, the old folks who lived next to Frank's old place. They'd seen pictures of lions lounging in downtown Nairobi and decided the trip would be too dangerous.

We can go on a TV safari any time, Makawee said. Besides, we're country folk. Nairobi would be way too big for us.

HAULANI TOWN

June 30, 2077

Haukea Haji
Global Regional Supervisory
Pacific Tectonic Islands Division
hhaji@GRS.global
Haulani Town
Big Island, HI
#globreg
Φ AmeraOneSatBx
virti_0123AllGlobal

Dear Ms. Haji,

Out of courtesy to you and hoping for an immediate virtiview or call or even a script, we're posting this communique in writing to you although in private. Now, 24 hours before we broadcast worldwide, yes, of course, worldwide, over my seventy-seven virti channels.

This is the Haulani Town Ethics Committee's eighth attempt to offer you time to resolve an enormous social problem that is symbolic of autocratic plutocratic dynastic assimilation.

My broadcast will be reviewed and NOT censored or hackalooed since all my channels including UHFA2865, CX39764, and all 75 others are approved and monitored by the Central North Pacific Supervisory Council as established by New World Council Decree 9726, 5cm, October 31,

2053 and licensed as free to all according to World Court Ruling 69511022856.

In case you don't recall or have never heard of us (you must have heard of us), Haulani Town is self-governed, self-owned, self-responsible within our available resource systems. The only criticism we've ever received as a community was from a new visitor who was frightened by some night groans and calls from the forest. We explained the noises came from our orangutan reserve. He was telling the ladies he was well fed, strong, and available. Our visitor was relieved. She thought the forest was haunted.

Haulani Town is peaceful and welcoming, to a fault. When Loihi first blew back in '42, we welcomed the scientists and the thrill seekers and invited several to settle nearby. We opened our Town to construction workers who we were fond us since their work on the shores of Loihi was meant to protect the Big Island from lava floods.

Despite our friendliness and tolerance, we're careful who we allow to stay more than a few months. If they nurture the Town in any way – food, fun, art, building, gardening, anything, kayak racing, surfing – we're happy to share our bit of paradise – before – Lono help us! - our island is absorbed in Loihi the way it's flowed over the atolls and Lanai and Kahoolawe.

One of the service people, Mr. Arnold Subodh Vigora, a registered Emotional Masseur, Lic. E.M., Ph.D,, came to Haulani Town at the invitation of the mayor. We expected he would address and maybe even heal the trauma lingering from the volcano's explosion and the total changes the expanding island brought to our lives.

Mr. Vigora was here for five years, then moved off island a year ago. He liquidated his Town assets, including a tiny mango farm, two houses, an antique canoe, and who knows what else. We understand he left Jany Mouilani, his partner, with a sizable debt they had incurred together.

Now he wants to come back on the same terms as when we first agreed to let him stay – because he claims he's a registered voter resident. Not true. He may be registered to vote, but has he ever?

Our terms allow true, approved residents the right to all the resources we take for granted. If the residents accepted for "Non-native but Good Person" status could not afford the fees, their portions are assessed to the wealthy residents who cheerfully contribute to Haulani Town's remaining serenity.

During his early years here, Mr. Vigora helped dozens of people adjust to living with the natural but terrible fear many felt just because they lived on the rim of a shaky tectonic plate, close to an island growing up and out like a teenage boy, and near another volcano that had been spewing fire and lava for decades. Many were lulled into the comforts of ignorance and denial even after Loihi burst into the air.

Mr. Vigora's clients gave him excellent recommendations, people liked him, and he made himself useful by offering Emotional Massages to all town employees gratis. A typical greedy billionaire, he was setting us up for his long-term takeover of Haulani town, we now understand.

As a so-called sustainable investor, his private foundation, InVigoRate Corp, has purchased nearly one-third of the land and houses in Town. Therefore, he insists, he has the right to return as a Non-native but Good Person with no financial, legal, or moral obligations.

For a long time, nobody here knew Vigora was the owner of InVigoRate Corp. We did finally admit to ourselves we should have looked into it when Bri Smithers, Alana Nakata, and Wisteria Chang all left their homes in the Town in the same week. Later we learned they had signed a contract with InVigoRate Corp that 1. Made them rich and 2. Swore them to keep silent about their sale for six months when they would receive the majority of their payments.

The rest of us agree Vigora can't just come back, shove his way into our lives, and do whatever he wants to do with his property and money. He says he'll be a good neighbor, but we don't trust him. He is a dry invasive species waiting to ignite.

It's true he did return to Haulani Town twice in the last two years to fulfill a Term of Work contract with his ex-partner. To Vigora's credit, Ms. Mouilani revealed she'd never experienced a more delicious and sweet time of affection than during his infrequent visits as he finished up his Term. Some of the best I've ever had, she said, under oath.

Such a recommendation for affectionate behavior is important to us but it will not justify his attempt to bully us. Nota bene: Ms. Mouilani also told us Vigora has no loyalty, no ability to commit, and no interest in working out the normal conflicts of a long-term relationship.

A sure proof of his fickleness and mendacity is the fact that, despite the fulfillment Vigora's ex-lover felt with him, she has taken up with a steady new friend, claiming disdain for Vigora (which also proves unique and emotionally overwhelming pleasures do not effect change as much as small regular satisfactions. This subject, in fact, is likely to be the topic of my upcoming November presentation to the Friends of Orangutan Society).

Haulani Town's core problem with Mr. Vigora is he plays fast and loose with the resources that belong to all of us, in common. His vast wealth could easily handle the food, water, oxygen, electricity costs the Town maintains through its community annuity and endowment funds. Not to mention his large security details and all their equipment. Not to mention we are really afraid he will buy out the Town endowment and boot us all off island, decades before the last surfer leaves and the Big Island is an arid plain of shiny black lava.

Also, please note, Ms. Haji, the fact that Joella Longsun (who you certainly know) of the Witness and Mediation Group division of the Global Regional Supervisors Office for the South Pacific Tectonic Islands in the Great Circle of Australia, Papua New Guinea, and Easter Island to our beloved and drowning in Loihi lava State of Hawaii, told us a mediated solution is possible but *highly unlikely.*

We do not want to take matters into our own hands, despite the pressure we feel from our relatives and friends of the Mauna Kea Protectors and Waimea Cowboy Associations. If we, or you, do not resolve this Vigora problem by the Autumn Equinox, I'm afraid even our diplomatic and political maneuvering skills will be of no avail. Nor can we in the Haulani Town Ethics Committee guarantee a continuing pacific life for Mr. Vigora, his allies, or his company.

This transition will not be virtual. It will be real and last as long as our beloved Town exists.

If it is up to us to undertake it, our hope is it will not be violent. Of course, that depends on Mr. Vigora. Your measures may be preferable due to their global signif-icance. Ours will certainly be final. And no, we are not afraid of Mr. Vigora, his troops, or his influence on the Supervisors Office, or above.

Act, please, Ms. Haji. After all, how much time do we have before Loihi spreads across the Big Island like mayonnaise on a sandwich and we say goodbye to the Place of the Gods, welcome the Place of Nowhere?

Speaking for the five native families, residents for 42,000 years and the seven new families, residents for 5 generations, I am

> Sincerely,
> Glorya Zhuk–Sky Atubukiro, Ph.D
> Director
> Haulani Town Ethics Committee
> Haulani Town, HI
> GZSABukiro@HTHI
> #VigoraProblem
> Virti among 365.33 – 6721.998

STEPS
OR
IT'S TOUGH TO OWN A BOOKSTORE

Bobbie and I go walking every Tuesday morning. We used to count our steps, always with 10,000 our goal. During the last couple of thousand we ran out of things to say – those last steps were always boring.

Now we turn around when we're still enthusiastic about the new neighbors with kids or her ideas (she has a new idea every week) about which city buildings should have murals or how the churches should come together to unite people from everywhere, rich and poor, all colors, whoever they are, to come here to live and be happy.

We would be a bubble of extravagant peace and freedom, she says.

This morning Bobbie was more serious than usual when she said, People are lazier than they used to be.

I hadn't noticed, I said.

O, yes, we are. We want everything delivered to their houses. You know, food, toilet paper, clothes, aspirin, books.

I had to admit I liked to have shoes and shirts show up right at my door.

Books, she said. Nobody wants to drive to the bookstore anymore. She stopped, looking around at the houses and the yards. Did you know that people are reading more than ever, only it's on their phones?

I didn't know that either, but I'd noticed the words on my phone take up a lot less space than in the newspaper or a book.

I forget almost everything I read on my phone, I told her, tapping my pocket where my phone slept.

Bobbie bent down to pick up a beer can from beside the street. She always carried a plastic bag to collect things stupid people threw out their car windows. Bobbie is a conscientious, environmental activist citizen. Some days, especially in April, she pulls on her gloves and fills two bags with nips, beer cans, soda bottles, Dunkin Donuts cups and straws, all junk revealed by spring's snow melt.

Books, she said as she hoisted her bag. It was only part-full because we walked here last week and the week before. Did you hear about the scandal at the bookstore?

I said, No. Tell me.

You know they had financial problems? Had to downsize to cards, kids books, tschotskes, a few graphic novels, paper-backs.

I checked my phone then and saw we'd come 3,989 steps, about halfway. I took her arm and we turned around. I'd been in the downsized bookstore and saw how small and tidy it was. I even bought some cute little animals made from some Hawaiian nuts.

Well, she said, they were in so deep they had to come up with some way to keep the lights on, so to speak. The wife began to flirt with the men who came in now and then and the husband began to charm the women who came in to browse, buy a romance novel or something. Most readers of books are women, you know.

Bobby spotted a Styrofoam cup hidden in the long grass of the yard by an abandoned house. The house looked in pretty good shape except for the lawn and a couple of shutters hanging askew.

I didn't know women are the main readers, I said. It makes sense. My watching baseball games or series about pirates or robot cowgirls doesn't leave me much time for reading.

Ignoring my feeble excuses for not reading, Bobbie said, Anyway, they would seduce the married customers and then blackmail them. That paid their bills for a year until they ran out of new people to seduce. Then they got desperate. They kidnapped the wife of a guy who owns a MacDonald's, a Cumberland Farms, and a Sunoco station. When he wouldn't pony up for his wife, the cops broke into the bookstore one night, freed the wife, and arrested the owners.

I'm a practical guy, a taxpayer and real aware of the town's economic health, so I asked her if anyone took over the store.

That's the best part, she said. A polygamous retiree and her two wives and three husbands bought it for almost nothing.

Hearing that made me happy. We still have a bookstore in town with owners who are probably too busy with each other to bother with kidnapping customers.

How are we doing with steps? Bobbie asked.

7,937.

Perfect, she said, as we approached our cars. I feel great.

As she opened her car door and set the trash bag down on the floor of back seat, I said, By the way, where does the expression 'pony up' come from?

She smiled and pointed to the phone in my hand.

I grinned, saying, I'll look it up.

As we drove away from our meeting place, I decided to visit the bookstore to check out the new owners. I was curious and I figured I could always buy a book or a magazine for Bobbie. I'd give it to her next Tuesday. She'd be pleased I bought local.

WHAT HAPPENED TO THE SKELETON WOMAN, THE HUNTER, AND THE INVISIBLE THIRD BEING

1. The Skeleton Woman

Clacking, scraping, she dragged her achy bones down the woods path to the sea. Tears poured over her cracked and furrowed cheeks. Her soft blue bonnet slipped off and tangled in her shoulder blades.

Eyes, she thought, My eyes grew back. I saw the sky, the fire in his hut, the oilskin slicker he wore. I looked into his dreams. I can't stop seeing all the pain he hid from my empty head.

Exhausted, dropping down the bank, she slid out onto the mud flat.

Eyes can go. I won't need them in the dark under the water. But the heart I will miss. It appeared like a scarlet pearl, soft as a rose forming around the tiny grain of desire I kept hidden from the salt all these years.

When he reached through my ribs, his fingers probing like fearless questions, I recoiled. The moment his touch grazed the wild flesh pulsing in my chest, I looked into his shining bwown eyes and I saw my true self. I collapsed. I fled to the comfort of mud.

In dim twilight, the Skeleton Woman lay tangled as a heap of old driftwood on the reeking mudflat, inviting the tide to come and scatter her across the bay.

2. The Hunter Returns to Hunting the Sea

After three days and nights, he awoke from a dreamless sleep. Lifting himself up from the icy floor of his cabin, he clutched the table, hauling his body up like the carcass of a seal.

Stumbling outside, he saw a trail scribbled in the piney woods path, a message he would never be able to read, but he understood it.

It's her, he thought. Gone back.

He loaded his boat with rope to tie her to him should he catch her, with his newest net, and with his three-pronged diamond-tipped silver narwhal hook. He tossed in an extra anchor.

His arms felt hot and numb at the same time. His fingertips were scorched. He launched into a night that his eyes saw as bright as noon because his whole body hummed with the blaze that had leapt from her heart to his. When they touched, flesh to flesh, his eyes really opened for the first time in his life. The shock of seeing his true self in her new eyes had knocked him out. Now the dim glow burned and beckoned him to the sea.

He rowed himself back and forth, dragging his net, peering into the opaque water until he nearly froze on the North Atlantic. And he came back day after day, just like always, never knowing what to expect, convinced he'd become braver.

3. The Invisible Third Being

If you could see her, you'd see someone as large as an adult and as heavy as two bodies. But since you can't see her, you can't see that she's as small as a kitten or rabbit.

She perched in the company of owls in a pine high over the mudflats where she observed Skeleton Woman gliding peacefully under the risen tide.

Waiting patiently for days and days, she watched the Hunter strain against the waves, dragging his net through the water, tugging it in, throwing it out, pulling it up, returning to land at night with an empty face whether he caught a bass or a flounder or nothing.

The Invisible Third Being drifted down to the water where she floated behind the Hunter, almost as visible as the shadow of a drifting cormorant. One morning, as the fog lifted, she rose up with the mist, and disappeared into open sky.

That day, a mysterious fragrance perfumed the breeze. A warm and wild scent of orchid called the Hunter ever further from shore. He caught sight of a pale fin rising and falling with the swells. It's her, he thought. I knew it.

He rowed on into the night.

CREDITS

Back Cover and page 18: Public domain photograph of "The Knotted Gun" by Carl Frederick Reuterswärd.

"The Knotted Gun" is a bronze sculpture of an oversized Colt Python .357 Magnum revolver with its muzzle tied in a knot. The sculpture is installed outside of the United Nations headquarters in New York.

According to Kofi Annan, the 7th Secretary-General of the United Nations:

It has enriched the consciousness of humanity with a powerful symbol that encapsulates, in a few simple curves, the greatest prayer of humanity; that which asks not for victory, but peace.

Since 1993, the sculpture has been the symbol of The Non-Violence Project Foundation, a nonprofit organization that promotes social change through violence-prevention education programs.

There are currently 31 copies of this sculpture around the world.

Page 70: Copyright Charles Schulz, "Peanuts"
Page 87: Photo of scene from "The Simpsons"
Page 116: "Purple Crocus" public domain Shutterstock
Page 138: Photo by Loretta Kane, "New Year's Eve"
Page 123: Photo, statue of Eleanor Roosevelt at the FDF Memorial, Washington, DC
Photos from random artists from the internet whose provenance was not available
Other photos selected from my personal photo library

BOOKS BY THOMAS TIMMINS

www.thomastimmins.com

Novels
  The Hour Between One and Two (Trilogy)
    Blood Medicine
    The Special Fruit Company
    Down at the River
  Aphrodisiac for an Angel
  The Silence of Frogs

Short Fiction
  Puff of Time
  Visions of My Other Self
  Desert Dusk Music
  Don't Worry - The Safety's On

Graphic Verse Novel
  Zom

Poetry
  Likings for Shadows
  I Was Just Laughing
  Food Breaks Free
  Almost Everyone
  some say yes
  Never Been Here Before
  between worlds
  card tricks
  Questions?
  3 little words

All profits from the sale of *Don't Worry - The Safety's On* will be donated to Sandy Hook Promise. **www.sandyhookpromise.org**

You can contribute to their gun control work at **takeaction.sandyhookpromise.org.**

www.ingramcontent.com/pod-product-compliance
Lightning Source LLC
Chambersburg PA
CBHW051951170626
46808CB00007B/2570